He had to do everything to get the babies out of there.

The sooner, the better.

"It'll be okay, right?" Darcy asked without taking her attention from the infrared.

"It will be." Nate tried to sound as convinced as he wanted to be.

"Noah will want his dinner soon," Darcy whispered.

Nate knew where she was going with this, and he figured it had to stop. They would drive themselves mad considering all the things that could go wrong. He glanced at her. But stopped.

He heard a sound.

A snap, as if someone had stepped on a twig.

Nate turned, trying to get the rifle into position. But it was already too late.

The man stepped through the wall of thick shrubs, and he aimed the gun right at Nate.

USA TODAY Bestselling Author

DELORES FOSSEN

NATE

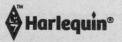

TM

Harlequin®

TORONTO NEW YORK LONDON
AMSTERDAM PARIS SYDNEY HAMBURG
STOCKHOLM ATHENS TOKYO MILAN MADRID
PRAGUE WARSAW BUDAPEST AUCKLAND

Recycling programs
for this product may
not exist in your area.

ISBN-13: 978-0-373-69591-1

NATE

Copyright © 2012 by Delores Fossen

ABOUT THE AUTHOR

Imagine a family tree that includes Texas cowboys, Choctaw and Cherokee Indians, a Louisiana pirate and a Scottish rebel who battled side by side with William Wallace. With ancestors like that, it's easy to understand why Texas author and former air force captain Delores Fossen feels as if she were genetically predisposed to writing romances. Along the way to fulfilling her DNA destiny, Delores married an air force top gun who just happens to be of Viking descent. With all those romantic bases covered, she doesn't have to look too far for inspiration.

Books by Delores Fossen

CAST OF CHARACTERS

Lt. Nate Ryland—When this widower's baby daughter is kidnapped, Nate must put his painful past behind him and join forces with the woman he considers his enemy. But battling the kidnappers is only the start. Nate also has to battle the fierce attraction for a woman he knows he should resist.

Darcy Burkhart—A defense attorney who's had legal battles with Nate. However, now they're not only on the same side, the stakes are sky high: their children's safety, their own lives and a possible relationship that could be the greatest risk of all.

Kimmie Ryland—Nate's fifteen-month-old daughter has been kidnapped from the Silver Creek Preschool and Day Care.

Noah Burkhart—Darcy's thirteen-month-old son and kidnap victim number two.

Willis Ramirez—A career criminal with a motive to go after Nate and Darcy.

Wesley Dent—A gold-digging artist who's under investigation for his wife's murder, and who might be linked to the preschool kidnapping.

Sandra Dent—This socialite's murder could be at the core of what happened at the preschool.

Edwin Frasier—Once married to the late Sandra Dent, he perhaps has the most powerful motive of all for the kidnapping.

Marlene Lambert—The day care assistant who's kidnapped along with Nate and Darcy's children.

Adam Frasier—Sandra Dent's rich, preppy son. He claims he's just trying to solve his mother's murder, but is he?

Chapter One

Lieutenant Nate Ryland took one look at the preschool building and knew something was wrong.

He eased his hand over his Glock. After ten years of being a San Antonio cop, it was an automatic response. But there was nothing rote or automatic about the iron-hard knot that tightened in his stomach.

"Kimmie," he said under his breath. His fifteen-month-old daughter, Kimberly Ellen, was inside.

The side door to the Silver Creek Preschool and Day Care was wide open. But not *just* open. It was dangling in place, the warm April breeze battering it against the sunshine-yellow frame. It looked as if it'd been partially torn off the hinges.

Nate elbowed his car door shut and walked closer. He kept his hand positioned over his gun and tried to rein in the fear that had started to crawl through him. He recognized the feeling. The sickening dread. The last time he'd felt like this he'd found his wife bleeding and dying in an alleyway.

Cursing under his breath, he hurried now, racing across the manicured lawn that was dotted with kiddie cars and other riding toys.

"What's wrong?" someone called out.

He snapped toward the voice and the petite brunette whom he recognized immediately. It wasn't a good recognition, either.

Darcy Burkhart.

A defense attorney who had recently moved to Silver Creek. But Nate had known Darcy before her move. Simply put, she had been and continued to be a thorn in his side. He'd already butted heads with her once today and didn't have time for round two.

Nate automatically scowled. So did she. She was apparently there to pick up her child. A son about Kimmie's age if Nate recalled correctly. He remembered Kimmie's nanny, Grace Borden, mentioning something about Darcy having enrolled the little boy in the two-hour-long Tuesday-Thursday play sessions held at the day-care center.

"I asked, what's wrong?" Darcy repeated. It was the same tone she used in court when representing the scum she favored defending.

Nate ignored both her scowl and her question, and continued toward the single-story building. The preschool was at the end of Main Street, nestled in a sleepy, parklike section with little noise or traffic. He reminded himself that it was a safe place for children.

Usually.

He had no idea what was wrong, but Nate knew that something was—the door was proof of that. He prayed there was a simple explanation for the damage. Like an ill-timed gust of wind. Or a preschool employee who'd given it too hard a push.

But it didn't feel like anything *simple*.

Without stopping, he glanced at the side parking lot. No activity there, though there were three cars, all belonging to the employees, no doubt. He also glanced behind him at the sidewalk and street where he and Darcy had left their own vehicles. If someone with criminal intentions had damaged the door, then the person wasn't outside.

That left the inside.

"Why is your hand on your gun?" Darcy asked, catching up with him. Not easily. She was literally running across the grassy lawn in high heels and a crisp ice-blue business suit, and the slim skirt made it nearly impossible for her to keep up with him.

"Shhhh," he growled.

Nate reached the front porch, which stretched across the entire front of the building. There were four windows, spaced far apart, and the nearest was still a few feet away from the door. He tested the doorknob.

It was locked.

Another sign that something was wrong. It was never locked this time of day because, like he had, other parents would arrive soon to pick up their children from the play session.

He drew his gun.

Behind him, Darcy gasped, and he shot her a get-quiet glare that he hoped she would obey. While he was hoping, he added that maybe she would stay out of the way.

She didn't.

Continuing to be a thorn in his side, she trailed along right behind him with those blasted heels battering like bullets on the wooden planks. Of course, he couldn't blame her. Her son was inside, and if she had any intuition whatsoever, she knew something wasn't right.

Nate moved to the window and peered around the

edge of the frame. He tried to brace himself for anything and everything but instead saw nothing. The room was empty.

Another bad sign.

It should literally be crawling with toddlers, the teacher and other staff members. This should be the last fifteen minutes of the play session, and the staff was expecting him. Nate had called an hour earlier to let them know that he would be arriving a little early so he could watch Kimmie play with the other kids. Maybe Darcy had had the same idea.

He lifted his head, listening, and it didn't take him long to hear the faint sound. Someone was crying. A baby. And it sounded like Kimmie.

Nothing could have held him back at that point. Nate raced across the porch and jumped over the waist-high railing so he could get to that door with the broken hinge. He landed on the ground, soggy from the morning's hard rain, and the mud squeezed over the toes of his cowboy boots. It seemed to take hours to go those few yards, but he finally made it. Unfortunately, the sound of the crying got louder and louder.

Nate threw open the broken door and faced yet another empty playroom. His heart went to his knees. Because the room wasn't just empty.

There were signs of a struggle.

Toys and furniture had been knocked over. There was a diaper bag discarded in the middle of the floor, and it looked as if someone had rifled through it. The phone, once mounted onto the wall, had been ripped off and now lay crushed and broken on the counter.

He didn't call out for his daughter, though he had to fight the nearly overwhelming urge to do just that and therefore alert a possible intruder. Kimmie had to be all right. She just had to be. Because the alternative was unthinkable. He'd already lost her mother, and he couldn't lose her.

Trying to keep his footsteps light so he would hopefully have the element of surprise, Nate made his way across the room and looked around the corner. No one was in the kitchen, but the crying was coming from the other side. It was one of the nap rooms, filled with beds and cribs, and normally it wasn't in use on Tuesday afternoons for the play group.

He heard the movement behind him, and with his Glock aimed and ready, he reeled around. It was Darcy, again. She gasped, and her cocoa-brown eyes widened at the gun pointed directly at her.

"Stay put," Nate whispered, using the hardest cop's expression he could manage. "Call nine-one-one and tell my brother to get out here."

Even though Darcy was new in town, she no doubt knew Sheriff Grayson Ryland was his brother. If she hadn't realized before there was something wrong, then she certainly knew it now.

"My son!" she said on a gasp.

She would have torn right past him if Nate hadn't snagged her arm. "Make the call," he ordered.

Her breath was gusting now, but she stopped struggling and gave a shaky nod. She rammed her hand into her purse and pulled out her cell phone.

Nate didn't wait for her to call the sheriff's office. She would do it, and soon Grayson and probably one of his other brothers would arrive. Two were deputies. And a nine-one-one call to respond to the preschool would get everyone in the sheriff's office moving fast.

Nate took aim again and hurried across the kitchen toward the nap room. The baby was still crying. Maybe it was Kimmie. But he heard something else, too. An adult's voice.

He stopped at the side of the door and glanced inside. At first, Nate didn't see the children. They weren't on the beds or in the cribs. But he looked down and spotted them.

Six toddlers.

They were huddled together in the corner with the teacher, Tara Hillman, and another woman Nate didn't recognize, but she no doubt worked there since both women wore name tags decorated with crayons. The babies were clinging to the adults, who were using hushed voices to try to comfort them.

"Lieutenant Ryland," Tara blurted out. Her eyes, like the other woman's, were red with tears, and they looked terrified.

With a baby clutched in each arm, Tara struggled to get to her feet. "Did you see them?"

"See who? What happened here?" Nate threaded his way through the maze of beds to make it to the other side of the room. He frantically looked through the huddle so he could find Kimmie.

"Two men," the other woman said. "They were wearing ski masks, and they had guns."

"They barged in before we could do anything to stop them," Tara explained.

"What happened here?" Nate repeated. He moved one of the babies aside. The one who was crying.

But it wasn't Kimmie.

"They took her," Tara said, though her voice hardly had any sound.

The words landed like fists against Nate and robbed him of his breath, maybe his sanity, too. "Took who?" He knew he was frantic now, but he couldn't stop himself.

"Kimmie." She made a hoarse sound. "They took Kimmie. Marlene, the other helper who works here, was holding her, and they made Marlene go with them. I couldn't stop them. I tried. I swear, I tried."

Everything inside Nate was on the verge of spinning out of control. That knot in his stomach moved to his throat and was choking him.

"What did they want? Where did they go?" he somehow managed to ask.

Tara swallowed hard and shook her head. "They drove away in a black van about ten minutes ago."

"Which direction?" Nate couldn't get out the question fast enough.

But Tara shook her head again. "They made us get on the floor, and I can't see the windows from there. They said if we went after them or if we called the sheriff that they'd come back and kill us all."

Nate turned to run. He had to get to his car *now*. He had to go in pursuit. He also had to get at least one of the deputies out to protect Tara and the babies just in case the gunmen followed through on their threat and returned. But he only made it a few steps before he smacked right into Darcy.

"They took Kimmie," he heard himself say.

But Darcy didn't seem to hear him. She was searching through the cluster of children. "Noah?" she called out. She repeated her son's name, louder this time.

Nate couldn't take the time to help her look. He had to find that van. He snatched his phone from his pocket and pressed the number for his brother. Grayson answered on the first ring.

"We're on the way," Grayson assured him without waiting for Nate to say a word. His brother had obviously gotten Darcy's call.

"According to the teacher, two armed men took Kimmie," Nate got out. "They kidnapped her and one of the workers, and they left in a black van. Close off the streets. Shut down the whole damn town before they have a chance to get out with her."

Nate didn't hear his brother's response because of the bloodcurdling scream that came from the preschool. That stopped him, and it wasn't more than a second or two before Darcy came tearing out of the building.

"They took Noah!" she yelled to Nate.

Hell. Not just one kidnapped child but two. "Did you hear?" Nate asked Grayson. He ran toward his car.

"I heard. So did Dade. He's listening in and already working to get someone out to look for that van. He'll get there in just a few minutes."

Dade, his twin brother and a Silver Creek deputy. Nate had no doubts that Dade would do everything he could to find Kimmie, but Nate wasn't going to just stand there and wait. He had to locate that van. He had to get Kimmie back.

"I'm going east," Nate let his brother know, and he ended the call so he could drive out of there fast.

Nate grappled to get the keys from his pocket, but his hands wouldn't cooperate. He tried to push the panic aside. He tried to think like a cop. But he wasn't just a cop. He was a father, and those armed SOBs had taken his baby girl.

He finally managed to extract his keys, somehow,

and he jerked open his car door. Nate jumped inside. But so did Darcy. She threw herself onto the passenger seat.

"I'm going with you," she insisted. "I have to get Noah."

"We don't even know who has them," Nate said. He dropped his cell phone onto the console between the seats so he could easily reach it. He needed it to stay in touch with Grayson.

"No, we don't know who has them, but they left this." She thrust a wrinkled piece of notebook paper at him. "It was taped to the side of the fridge."

Nate looked at her, trying to read her expression, but he only saw the fear and worry that was no doubt on his own face. He took the paper and read the scrawled writing.

This was his worst nightmare come true.

Nate Ryland and Darcy Burkhart, we have them. Cooperate or you'll never see your babies again.

Chapter Two

Cooperate or you'll never see your babies again.

The words raced through Darcy's head. She wanted
to believe this wasn't really happening, that any second
now she would wake up and see her son's smiling face.
But the crumpled letter in Nate Ryland's hand seemed
very real. And so was the fear that bubbled up in her
throat.

"Cooperate?" she repeated. "How?"

There were a dozen more questions she could have
added to those, but Nate didn't seem to have any more
answers than she did. The only thing that appeared certain right now was that two gunmen had taken Nate's
daughter, her son and a preschool employee, and they
had driven off in a black van.

Nate's breath was gusting as much as hers, and he
had a wild look in his metal-gray eyes. Even though his
hands were shaking and he had a death grip on his gun,
he managed to start his car, and he sped off, heading
east, away from the center of town.

"This is the way the kidnappers went?" Darcy asked,
praying that he knew something she didn't.

He dropped the letter next to his cell phone. "We
have a fifty-fifty chance they did."

Oh, God. That wasn't nearly good enough odds when it came to rescuing Noah. "I should get in my car and go in the opposite direction. That way we can cover both ends of town."

"Grayson will do that," Nate snarled. He aimed a glare at her. "Besides, what good would you do going up against two armed men?"

"What good could I do?" Darcy practically yelled. "They have my son, and I'll get him back." Even though she didn't have a gun or any training in how to fight off bad guys. Still, she had a mother's love for her child, and that could overcome anything.

She hoped.

"You'll get yourself killed and maybe the children hurt," Nate fired back. "I'm not going to let you do that." And it wasn't exactly a suggestion.

He was right, of course. She hated that, but it was true. Even if she managed to find the van, she stood little chance of getting past two armed men, especially since she didn't want to give them any reason to fire shots. Not with her baby in that vehicle.

Nate flew past the last of the buildings but then slammed on the brakes. For a moment she thought he'd spotted the van. But no such luck. He was stopping for the dark blue truck that was coming from the opposition direction.

"My brother Dade," Nate told her. "He might have some news that'll help us narrow the search."

Good. She was aware that Nate had a slew of brothers, all in law enforcement. And she was also aware that Dade was a deputy sheriff since only two months earlier he'd been involved in the investigation of one of her former clients. A client killed in a shoot-out with Nate.

The two vehicles screeched to a stop side by side, and both men put down the windows. Darcy ducked down a little so she could see the man in the driver's seat of the truck.

Yes, definitely Nate's brother.

He had the same midnight-black hair. The same icy eyes. But Dade looked like a rougher version of his brother, who had obviously just come from his job in SAPD. Nate wore jeans but with a crisp gray shirt and black jacket. Dade looked as if he'd just climbed out of the saddle, with his denim shirt and battered Stetson.

The brothers exchanged glances. Brief ones. But it felt as if a thousand things passed silently between them. "Anything?" Nate asked.

Dade's troubled eyes conveyed his answer before he even spoke. "Not yet."

"There was a note," Nate said, handing it through the window to his brother. He immediately started to slap the fingers of his left hand on the steering wheel. He was obviously eager to leave and so was Darcy. "Later I need it bagged and checked for prints."

Later. After they'd rescued the children. Darcy didn't want to think beyond that.

"Once one of the other deputies arrives at the pre-school, I'll be out to help you look," Dade offered. "Was anyone in the building hurt?"

Nate shook his head. "It looked like a smash and grab. Entry through the side door. No signs of...blood."

Dade returned the nod. "Good. Hang in there. We'll find these goons, and we'll find Kimmie."

Nate gave Dade one last brief look, maybe to thank

him, and he hit the accelerator again. He sped off in the opposite direction of his brother while he fired glances all around. He wasn't just checking Main Street but all of the side roads and parking lots.

Silver Creek wasn't a large town, but there was a solid quarter mile of shops and houses on Main Street. And there were no assurances that the kidnappers would stay on the main road. Most of the side streets wound their way back to the highway, and that terrified her. Because if the kidnappers made it to the highway, it was just a few miles to the interstate.

"I have to do something," she mumbled. Darcy couldn't stop the panic. Nor the fear. It was building like a pressure cooker inside her as Nate sped past each building.

"You can do something." Nate's voice was strained, like the muscles in his face. "You can keep watch for that van and try to figure out why those men did this."

That didn't settle the panic, but it did cause her to freeze. Why had those men done this? Why had they specifically taken Nate's daughter and her son?

"You're a cop," she blurted out. "This could be connected to something you've done. Maybe someone has a grudge because you arrested him." It was a possible motive. And that caused anger to replace some of the panic. "This could be your fault."

It wasn't reasonable, but by God she wasn't in a reasonable kind of mood. She wanted her son back.

Nate kept his attention nailed to the road, but he also scowled. He clearly wasn't pleased with her accusation. Or with her. But then he always scowled when she was around.

"If this is my fault, then why did they take your son?" Nate asked.

She opened her mouth to explain that away, but she couldn't. Darcy could only sit there and let that sink in. It didn't sink in well.

"If I counted right, there were eight toddlers in that play group today. Eight," he spat out with his teeth semi-clenched. "And they only took ours. They said cooperate or we'd never see our babies again. *Our babies,*" he emphasized. "So what the devil did you do to bring this down on us? You're the one who likes to muck around with slime."

She shook her head, trying to get out the denial. Yes, she was a defense attorney. She'd even successfully defended the man who'd originally been arrested for masterminding the murder of Nate's wife. But that was resolved. His wife's killer was now dead, and so was her former client Charles Brennan.

But he hadn't been her only client.

In the past she had indeed defended people with shady reputations, and in some cases she hadn't been successful. Maybe one of those less-than-stellar clients was holding a grudge.

Oh, mercy. Nate was right. This could all be her fault.

The tears came. She'd been fighting them from the moment she realized something was wrong in the preschool, but she lost that fight now.

"I need you to keep watch," Nate growled. "You can't do that if you're crying, so dry your eyes and help me look for that van."

"But this is my fault." She tried to choke back a sob but failed at that, too.

"Stop thinking like a mother for just a second. They took both children so it's connected to both of us. Not just me. Not just you. *Both*."

Her gaze flew to his, and she met his frosty-metal eyes. The raw emotions of the moment were still there, deep in those shades of gray, but she could also see the cop now. Here was the formidable opponent she'd come up against in the past.

"The man who killed your wife is dead," she reminded him. "And so is the person who hired him."

"Wesley Dent isn't in jail," Nate provided. He took his attention off her and put it back on the road.

Yes. Wesley Dent was her client. A San Antonio man under investigation for poisoning his wife. Dent had retained her a few days after his wife's death because he was concerned about the accusatory tone the police were taking with him. She'd accompanied him to several interviews and had successfully argued to put limits on the search warrant that was being issued for his house and vehicles.

And the lead investigator in the case was none other than Nate.

Darcy gave that some thought and shook her head. "I don't think Wesley Dent would do this. I'm not even sure he's capable of poisoning anyone."

"He's guilty," Nate said with the complete confidence that only a cop could have.

Darcy was far from convinced of that, but to the best of her knowledge, Dent was the only thing that connected Nate and her. Still, it didn't matter at this point if Dent was the one responsible. They needed to find the van.

Nate's cell phone rang, and without picking it up, he jabbed the button to answer the call on speaker.

"It's Grayson," the caller said.

The sheriff, and from what she'd heard, a very capable lawman. Darcy held her breath, praying that he had good news.

"Anything?" Nate immediately asked.

"No. But we're putting everything in place." He paused just a second. "Dade said you have Ms. Burkhart in the vehicle with you."

"Yeah. She jumped in as I was driving away."

The sheriff mumbled something she didn't catch, but it sounded like profanity. "I shouldn't have to remind you that if you find this van, you should wait for backup. You two shouldn't try to do this alone."

Nate paused, too. "No, we shouldn't. But if I see that van, nothing is going to stop me. Just make sure you have a noose around the area. I don't want them getting away."

"They won't. Now, tell me about this note you gave Dade."

"It said, 'Nate Ryland and Darcy Burkhart, we have them. Cooperate or you'll never see your babies again.' And yes, I know what that means." Nate tightened his grip on the steering wheel. "They won't harm the children because they want them for leverage. I think this is connected to a man named Wesley Dent. Call my captain and have Dent brought in for questioning. Beat the truth out of him if necessary."

Darcy knew she should object to that. She believed in the law with her whole heart. But her son's safety suddenly seemed above the law.

"I don't suppose it'd do any good to ask you to come

back to the station," Grayson said. "We have plenty of people out looking for the van."

"I'm not coming back. Not until—" Nate's eyes widened, and she followed his gaze to what had grabbed his attention.

Oh, mercy. There was a black van on the side street. It was moving but not at a high speed.

Noah could be in there.

"I just spotted the possible escape vehicle on Elmore Road," Nate relayed to his brother. "It's on the move, and I'm in pursuit."

Nate turned his car on what had to be two wheels at most, and with the tires squealing, he maneuvered onto the narrow road. There were houses here, spaced far apart, but thankfully there didn't seem to be any other traffic. Good thing, too, because Nate floored the accelerator and tore through the normally quiet neighborhood.

So did the driver of the van.

He sped up, which meant he had no doubt seen them. Not that she'd expected them to be able to sneak up on the vehicle, but Darcy had hoped they would be able to get closer so she could look inside the windows.

Nate read off the license-plate number to his brother, who was still on the line, though she could hear the sheriff making other calls. Grayson was assembling backup for Nate. She only prayed they wouldn't need it, that they could resolve this here and now.

"Can you try to shoot out the tires or something?" she asked.

"Not with the kids inside. Too risky."

Of course, it was. She obviously wasn't thinking

clearly and wouldn't until she had her baby safely in her arms. "How will we get it to stop?"

"Grayson will have someone at the other end of this road. Once the guy realizes he can't escape, he'll stop."

Maybe. And maybe that shoot-out would happen, after all. Darcy tried not to give in to the fear, but she got a double dose of it when the van sped over a hill and disappeared out of sight.

"Are there side roads?" she asked. She'd never been on Elmore or in this particular part of Silver Creek.

"Yeah. Side roads and old ranch trails."

That didn't help with the fear, and she held her breath until Nate's car barreled over the hill. There, about a quarter of a mile in front of them, she could see the van. But not for long. The driver went around a deep curve and disappeared again.

It seemed to take hours for Nate to reach that same curve, and he was going so fast that he had to grapple with the steering wheel to remain in control. The tires on her side scraped against the gravel shoulder and sent a spray of rocks pelting into the car's undercarriage. It sounded like gunshots, and that made her terror worse.

They came out of the curve, only to go right into another one. Nate seemed to realize it was coming because he was already steering in that direction.

Darcy prayed that it wouldn't be much longer before Grayson or someone else approached from the other side of the road so they could stop this chase. She didn't want to risk the van crashing into one of the trees that dotted the sides of the road.

She could hear the chatter on Nate's cell, which was still on speaker. People were responding. Everything was in motion, but the truth was Nate and she were the ones who were closest to the van. They were their children's best bet for rescue.

"Hold on," Nate warned as he took another turn. "And put on your seat belt."

Her hands were shaking, but she managed to get the belt pulled across her. She was still fumbling with the latch when their car came out of yet another curve followed by a hill.

The moment they reached the top of the hill, she saw the van.

And Darcy's heart went to her knees.

"Stop!" she yelled.

Nate was already trying to do just that. He slammed on the brakes. But they were going too fast. And the van was sideways, right in the middle of the road. The vehicle wasn't moving, and there was no way for Nate to avoid it.

Darcy screamed.

Just as they crashed head-on into the black van.

Chapter Three

Nate heard the screech of his brakes as the asphalt ripped away at the tires. There was nothing he could do.

Nothing.

Except pray and try to brace himself for the impact.

He didn't have to wait long.

The car slammed into the van, tossing Darcy and him around like rag dolls. The air bags deployed, slapping into them and sending a cloud of the powdery dust all through the car's interior.

It was all over in a split second. The whiplashing impact. The sounds of metal colliding with metal.

Nate was aware of the pain in his body from having his muscles wrenched around. The mix of talc and cornstarch powder from the air bag robbed him of what little breath he had. But now that he realized he had survived the crash, he had one goal.

To get to the children.

Nate prayed they hadn't been hurt.

He lifted his head, trying to listen. He didn't hear anyone crying or anyone moaning in pain. That could be good.

Or very bad.

Next to him, Darcy began to punch at the air bag that

had pinned her to the seat. He glanced at her, just to make sure she wasn't seriously injured. She had a few nicks on her face from the air bag, and her shoulder-length dark brown hair was now frosted with the talc mixture, but she was fighting as hard as he was to get out of the vehicle. No doubt to check on her son.

"When we get out, stay behind me and let me do the talking," Nate warned her.

Though he doubted his warning would do any good. If the kidnappers hadn't been injured or, better yet, incapacitated, then this was going to get ugly fast.

Nate got a better grip on his gun and opened his door. Or rather, that's what he tried to do. The door was jammed, and he had to throw his weight against it to force it open. He got out, his boots sinking into the soggy shoulder of the road, and got a good look at the damage. The front end of his car was a mangled heap, and it had crumpled the side of the van, creating a deep V in the exterior.

Still no sounds of crying. In fact, there were no sounds at all coming from the van.

"I'm Lieutenant Nate Ryland," he called out. "Release the hostages *now!*"

He waited, praying that his demand wouldn't be answered with a hail of bullets. Anything he did right now was a risk and could make it more dangerous for the children, but he couldn't just stand there. He had to try something to get Kimmie and Noah away from their kidnappers.

In the distance he could hear a siren from one of the sheriff department's cruisers. The sound was coming from the opposite direction so that meant Grayson or one of the other deputies would soon be there. But Nate didn't intend to wait for backup to arrive. His daughter could be hurt inside that van, and he had to check on her.

Darcy finally managed to fight her way out of the wrecked car, and she hit the ground running. Or rather, limping. However, the limping didn't stop her. She went straight for the van. Nate would have preferred for her to wait until he'd had time to assess things, but he knew there was no stopping her, not with her son inside.

"Noah?" she shouted.

Still no answer.

That didn't stop Darcy, either, and she would have thrown open the back doors of the van if Nate hadn't stepped in front of her and muscled her aside. This could be an ambush with the kidnappers waiting inside to gun them down, but these SOBs obviously wanted Darcy and him for something. Maybe that *something* meant they would keep them alive.

"Kimmie?" Nate called out, and he cautiously opened the van doors while he kept his gun aimed and ready.

It took him a moment to pick through the debris and the caved-in side, but what he saw had him cursing.

No one was there. Not in the seats, not in the back cargo area. Not even behind the wheel.

A sob tore from Darcy's mouth, and if Nate hadn't caught her, she likely would have collapsed onto the ground.

"Where are they?" she begged. And she just kept repeating it.

Nate glanced all around them. There were thick woods on one side of the road and an open meadow on the other. The grass didn't look beaten down on the meadow side so that left the woods. He shoved his hand over Darcy's mouth so he could hear any sounds. After all, two gunmen and three hostages should be making lots of sounds.

But he heard nothing other than Darcy's frantic mumbles and the approaching siren.

"They were here," Nate said more to himself than Darcy, but she stopped and listened. He took the hand from her mouth. "That's Kimmie's diaper bag." It was lying right against the point of impact.

"And that's Noah's bear," Darcy said, reaching for the toy.

Nate pulled her back. Yes, the children had likely been here, but so had the kidnappers. The diaper bag and the toy bear might have to be analyzed. Unless Nate found the children and kidnappers first.

And that's exactly what he intended to do.

"Wait here," he told Darcy. "I need to figure out where they went." He tried not to think of his terrified baby being hauled through the woods by armed kidnappers, but he knew it was possible.

By God when he caught up to these men, they were going to pay, and pay hard.

"Look!" Darcy shouted.

Nate followed the direction of her pointing index finger and spotted the name tag. It was identical to the ones he'd seen Tara and the other woman wearing in the preschool. This one had the name Marlene Lambert, a woman he'd known his whole life. Her father's ranch was just one property over from his family's.

"The name tag looks as if it was ripped off her," Darcy mumbled.

Maybe. It wasn't just damaged—one of the four crayons had been removed. He glanced around the name tag and spotted the missing yellow crayon. It was right at the base of the rear doors.

"She wrote something." Darcy pointed to the left door at the same moment Nate's attention landed on it.

There was a single word, three letters, scrawled on the metal, but Nate couldn't make out what it said. Later, he would try to figure it out, but for now he raced away from the van and to the edge of the road that fronted the woods.

Nate didn't see any footprints or any signs of activity so he began to run, looking for anything that would give them a clue where the children had been taken. Darcy soon began to do the same and went in the opposite direction.

He glanced up when Dade's truck squealed to a stop. His brother had put the portable siren on top of his truck, but thankfully now he turned it off. Unlike Darcy and Nate, Dade was coming from a straight part of the road and had no doubt seen the collision in time. That was why Nate hadn't bothered to go back to his car and try to retrieve his cell phone so he could alert whoever would be coming from that direction.

"They're not inside," Nate relayed to his brother, and he kept looking.

Dade cursed. "There's a helicopter on the way," he let Nate know. "And I'll call the Rangers and get a tracker out here. Mason, too," Dade added the same moment that Nate said their brother's name.

Mason was an expert horseman, and he was their best bet at finding the children in these thick woods. First, though, Nate needed to find the point at which they'd left the road. That would get him started in the right direction.

And he finally found it.

Footprints in the soft shoulder of the road.

"Here!" he called out to his brother. But Nate didn't wait for Dade to reach him. Nor did he follow directly in the footsteps. He hurried to the side in case the prints were needed for evidence, and there were certainly a lot of them if castings were needed.

But something was wrong.

Hell.

"There's only one set of footprints," Nate relayed to Dade.

Dade cursed too and fanned out to Nate's left, probably looking for more prints. There should be at least three sets since the adults would be carrying the babies.

"The person who made this set of prints could be a diversion," Nate concluded, and he hurried to the other side of the road, hoping to find the real trail there.

Darcy quickly joined him. She was still limping, and blood was trickling down the side of her head. He hoped like the devil she wasn't in need of immediate medical attention or on the verge of a panic attack. He needed her help, her eyes, because these first few minutes were critical.

"Go that way," Nate instructed, pointing in the opposite direction where he intended to look.

He ran, checking each section of the pasture for any sign that anyone had been there. He knew the kidnappers weren't on the road itself because Darcy and he had come from one end and Dade the other. If two kidnappers and three hostages had been anywhere near the road, they would have seen them.

Nate made it about a hundred yards from the collision site when he heard Dade's cell ring. He didn't stop looking, but he tried to listen, hoping that his brother was about to get good news. Judging from the profanity Dade used, he hadn't.

"This van's a decoy," Dade shouted.

Nate stopped and whirled around. Darcy did the same and began to run back toward Dade. "What do you mean?"

"I mean two other eyewitnesses spotted black vans identical to this one."

Darcy made it to Dade, and she latched on to his arm. "But there's proof the children were inside. Noah's bear and Kimmie's diaper bag. Marlene's name tag is there, too."

Dade looked at Nate when he answered. "This was probably the van initially used in the kidnapping, but the children and Marlene were transferred to another vehicle. Maybe they were even split up since at least two other vans were seen around town."

Nate had already come to that conclusion, and it made him sick to his stomach. He couldn't choke back the groan. Nor could he fight back the overwhelming sense of fear.

"If they split up, then there are probably more than two of them," Nate mumbled.

That meant things had gone from bad to worse. The kidnappers could have an entire team of people helping them, and heaven knows what kind of vehicle they had used to transfer the children.

Nate was betting it wasn't a black van.

It could have been any kind of vehicle. Darcy and

he could have driven right past the damn thing and wouldn't have even noticed it.

"We have people out on the roads," Dade reminded them. "More are coming in. And there's an Amber Alert and an APB out on the van. SAPD and all other law-enforcement officers in the area will stop any van matching the description. We'll find them, Nate. I swear, we'll find them."

Nate checked his watch. About twenty minutes had passed. That was a lifetime in a situation like this. The kidnappers could already have reached the interstate.

"I'll take you back to the sheriff's office," Dade insisted. He glanced down at Darcy. In addition to the nicks on her face, her jacket was torn, and there were signs of a bruise on her knee. "You need to see a medic."

"No!" she practically shouted. "I need to find my baby."

But the emotional outburst apparently drained her because the tears came, and Nate hooked his arm around her waist. He didn't feel much like comforting her, or anyone else, for that matter, but the sad truth was there was only one person who knew exactly how he felt.

And that was Darcy.

She sagged against him and dropped her head on his shoulder. "We have to keep looking," she begged.

"We will." Nate looked at his brother. "We need another vehicle. And I need to call the San Antonio crime lab so they can come out and collect this van." Silver Creek didn't have the CSI capabilities that SAPD did, and Nate wanted as many people on this as possible.

Nate adjusted Darcy's position so he could get her

moving to Dade's truck, but he stopped when he took another look at the scrawled letters written in yellow crayon. He eased away from Darcy and walked closer.

"You think Marlene wrote that?" Dade asked.

Nate nodded. "She might have tried to leave us a message." He studied those three letters. *"L-A-R,"* he read aloud.

"Lar?" Dade shook his head, obviously trying to figure it out, too.

"Maybe it's someone's initials," Darcy suggested. She moved between Dade and Nate, and leaned in. "Maybe she's trying to tell us the identity of the person who took her."

It was possible. Of course, that would mean it wasn't Wesley Dent, and it would also mean Marlene had known her kidnapper. That possibility tightened the knot in Nate's stomach. But there was something more here.

Something familiar.

Dade rattled off names of people who might fit those initials. He only managed two—an elderly couple with the last name of Reeves. Nate figured neither was capable of this. But his own surname began with an *R*.

Did that mean anything?

"A street name, then," Darcy pressed.

Dade lifted his phone and snapped a picture. "Come on. Let's go. We'll try to work it out on the drive back to the sheriff's office."

It was a good plan, but Nate couldn't take his attention off those three letters. They were familiar, something right on the tip of his tongue.

"Let's go," Darcy urged. She tugged on Nate's arm to get him moving.

They only made it a few steps before Nate heard a phone ring. Not Dade's. The sound was coming from his wrecked car, and it was his phone. He hurried toward it, but it stopped ringing just as he got there. He located his cell in the rubble and saw the missed call.

The number and caller's identity had been blocked.

Hell. It had probably been the kidnappers. "It could have been the ransom call."

"Try to call them back," Darcy insisted. But the words had hardly left her mouth when another phone rang. "That's my cell." She frantically tore through the debris to locate her purse. She jerked out the phone and jabbed the button to answer it.

She pressed the phone to her ear, obviously listening, but she didn't say a word. When the color drained from her face, Nate moved closer.

"But—" That was all she managed to say.

Nate wanted the call on speaker so he could hear, but he couldn't risk trying to press any buttons on her phone. He darn sure didn't want to disconnect the call. All he could do was wait.

"I want my son. Give me back my son!" she shouted. The tears welled up in her eyes and quickly began to spill down her cheeks. Several seconds later, Darcy's hand went limp, the phone dropping away from her ear.

Nate snatched the phone from her, but the call had already ended.

"Who was it and what did they say?" Nate demanded. He caught her by the shoulders and positioned her so that it forced eye contact.

She groaned and shook her head. "The person had a mechanical voice, like he was speaking through some kind of machine, but I think it was a man. He said he had the children and Marlene and that if we wanted them back, he would soon be in touch. Then he hung up."

"That's it? That's all he said?" Nate tried to calm down but couldn't. "He didn't say if the kids were safe?"

"No," she insisted.

Nate took her phone. He tried the return-call function on his cell first. It didn't go through. Instead he got a recording about the number no longer being in service. The same thing happened when he tried to retrieve the call from Darcy's phone.

A dead end.

But maybe it was just a temporary one.

Dade gathered both cells. "I'll see if we can get anything about the caller from these. Darcy, you need to write down everything you can remember from that conversation because each word could be important."

She nodded and smeared the tears from her cheeks. "Let's get that other vehicle so we can look for them."

Nate agreed, but he stopped and stared at the three letters written on the door of the van.

LAR.

"I already have a picture of it," Dade reminded him. "You can study it later."

Nate cursed. "I don't need to study it." He started to run toward Nate's truck. "I know what Marlene is trying to tell us. I know where we can find the children."

Chapter Four

"LAR," Darcy said under her breath.

Lost Appaloosa Ranch.

Well, maybe that's what the initials meant. Of course, Nate could be wrong, and it could turn out to be a wild-goose chase. A chase that could cost them critical time because it tied up manpower that could be directed somewhere other than the remote abandoned ranch. According to Nate, the owner had died nearly a year ago, and his mortgage lender was still trying to contact his next of kin.

"Hurry," Darcy told the medic again. And yes, she glared at him. She'd spent nearly fifteen minutes in the Silver Creek sheriff's office, and that was fifteen minutes too long.

Darcy didn't want to be here. She wanted to be out looking for Noah, but instead here she was, sitting at the sheriff's desk while a medic stitched her up. God knows how she'd gotten the cut right on her hairline, and she didn't care.

She didn't care about anything but her son.

"I'm trying to hurry," the medic assured her.

She knew from his name tag that he was Tommy Watters, and while she hated being rude to him, she couldn't stop herself. She had to do something. *Anything.*

Like Nate and his four brothers were doing.

Just a few yards away from her, Nate was on the phone, his tone and motions frantic, while he talked with the helicopter pilot, who was trying to narrow down the search zone.

"No," Nate instructed. "Don't do a direct fly over the Lost Appaloosa. I already have someone en route, and if the kidnappers are there, I don't want to alert them. I want you to focus on the roads that lead to the interstate."

Nate had a map spread out on the desk, and every line on the desk phone was blinking. Next door, Deputy Melissa Garza was barking out orders to a citizens' patrol group that was apparently being formed to assist in the hunt for the kidnappers and the babies. The dispatcher was helping her.

Grayson, Dade and Mason were all out searching various parts of Silver Creek, interviewing witnesses and running down leads on the other black vans that had been spotted. The other deputy, Luis Lopez, was at the day care in case the kidnappers returned.

Darcy was the only one not doing anything to save Noah and Kimmie.

"I can't just sit here." The panic was starting to whirl around inside her, and despite the AC spilling over her, sweat popped out on her face. She would scream if she couldn't get out of there and find Noah.

Darcy pushed aside the medic and would have run out of the room if Nate hadn't caught her shoulder.

He got right in her face, and his glare told her this wasn't going to be a pep talk. "You have to keep yourself together. Because I don't have time to babysit you. Got that?"

She flinched. That stung worse than the fresh stitches. But Darcy still shook her head. "Noah is my life." Which, of course, went without saying. Kimmie was no doubt Nate's life, too.

Nate nodded, and eased up on the bruising grip he had on her shoulder. The breath he blew out was long and weary. He looked up at the medic as he put Darcy back in the chair. "Finish the stitches *now,*" he ordered.

Actual fear went through the medic's eyes, and he clipped off the thread. "It'll hold for now, but she should see a doctor because she might have a concussion."

Before the last word left the medic's mouth, Darcy was out of the chair. "Let's go," she insisted.

Thank God, Nate didn't argue with her. "We're headed to the Lost Appaloosa, Mel," he shouted to Deputy Garza, and in the same motion Nate grabbed a set of keys from a hook on the wall.

Finally! They were getting out there and doing something. She hoped it was the *right* something.

"You have to keep yourself together," Nate repeated. But this time, there was no razor edge to his tone. No glare. Just speed. He practically ran down the hall. "My brother Kade should arrive at the Lost Appaloosa in about ten minutes, and then we'll have answers."

"Answers *if* the babies are really there," Darcy corrected.

Nate spared her a glance, threw open the back door and hurried into the parking lot. "Marlene probably risked her life to write those initials. They mean something, and if it turns out to be the Lost Appaloosa, then Kade will know how to approach the situation."

"Because he's FBI," she said more to herself than Nate.

Darcy prayed Nate's FBI brother truly knew what he was doing. It gave her some comfort to know that Kade would likely be willing to risk his life to save his niece. And maybe Noah, too.

Nate jumped into a dark blue SUV, started the engine and barely waited long enough for Darcy to get inside before he tore out of the parking lot.

"I need to know if you're okay," he said, tipping his head to her new stitches.

"Don't worry about me," Darcy said. "Focus on the kids."

"I can't have you keeling over or anything." The muscles in his jaw stirred. Maybe because he didn't like that he had to be concerned about her in any way.

"I'm fine," she assured him, and even though it was a lie, it was the end of the discussion as far as Darcy was concerned. "How far is the Lost Appaloosa?"

"Thirty miles. It's within the San Antonio city limits, but there's not much else out there." His phone buzzed, and he shoved it between his shoulder and ear when he answered it.

She listened but couldn't tell anything from Nate's monosyllabic responses. He certainly wasn't whooping for joy because the babies had possibly been found.

Darcy leaned over to check the odometer so she would know when they were close to that thirty miles, and her hair accidently brushed against Nate's arm. He glanced at it, at her, and Darcy quickly pulled away.

"Thirty miles," she repeated, focusing on the drive and not on the driver. Nate put his attention back on the call.

That was too many miles between her and her baby, and the panic surged through her again. Nate was already going as fast as he could, but at this speed and because of the narrow country roads, it would take them at least twenty, maybe twenty-five, minutes to get there.

An eternity.

Nate cursed, causing her attention to snap back to him. She waited, breath held, until he slapped the phone shut. "Grayson just found another empty black van on a dirt road near the creek. Only one set of footprints was around the vehicle."

So, not a call from Kade. Just news of another decoy van. Or else the team of kidnappers had split up. Did that mean they'd split up the children and Marlene, as well? Darcy hoped not.

"Shouldn't you have heard from Kade by now?" she asked.

He scrubbed his hand over his face. "My brother will call when he can."

Nate looked at her again, and his eyes were now a dangerous stormy-gray. "The person behind this has a big motive and a lot of money," he tossed out there. He was all cop again. Here was the lieutenant she'd butted heads with in the past. And the present.

"You mean Wesley Dent," she supplied.

Darcy didn't even try to put on her lawyer face. Her head was pounding. Her breath, ragged. And her heart was beating so hard, she was afraid her ribs might crack. She didn't have the energy for her usual power-attorney facade.

"Wesley Dent," Nate verified, making her client's name sound like profanity. "He's a gold digger, and I believe he murdered his wife."

Darcy shook her head and continued to keep watch in case she spotted another black van. She also glanced at the odometer, remembering to keep her hair away from Nate's arm. Twenty-five miles to go.

"I won't deny the gold-digging part," she admitted, "but I'm not sure he killed his wife."

Though it did look bad for Dent.

A starving artist, Dent had married Sandra Frasier, who wasn't just a multimillionaire heiress but was twenty-five years his senior. And apparently she often resorted to public humiliation when it came to her boy-toy husband, who was still two years shy of his thirtieth birthday. Just days before what would have been their first wedding anniversary, Sandra had humiliated Dent in public at Dent's art show.

A day after that, she had received a lethal dose of insulin.

"Sandra was diabetic," Darcy continued, though she really didn't want to have this conversation. Twenty-four miles to go. "So, it's possible this was a suicide. Her husband even said she wrote about suicide in her diary." But her death certainly hadn't been accidental because the amount of insulin was quadruple what she would have normally taken.

"There was no suicide note," Nate challenged. "No sign of this so-called diary, either."

But that didn't mean the diary didn't exist. Dent had told her that his wife kept it under lock and key, so maybe she'd moved it so that no one would be able to read her intimate thoughts.

"The husband is often guilty in situations like this," Nate went on. He had such a hard grip on the steering wheel that his knuckles were white. "And I think Dent could have orchestrated this kidnapping to force me to stop the investigation. I'm within days of arresting his sorry butt for murder."

Darcy wished the pain in her head would ease up a little so she could think straighter. "There are other suspects," she reminded him.

"Yeah, the dead woman's ex-husband and her son, but neither has as strong a motive as Dent."

"Maybe," Darcy conceded. Another glance at the odometer. Twenty-three miles between the ranch and them. "But if Dent masterminded this kidnapping to stop the investigation, then why take Noah? I'm his lawyer, the one person who could possibly prevent him from being arrested."

Nate shook his head, cursed again. "Maybe he thinks if he has your son that you'll put pressure on me to cooperate."

She opened her mouth to argue, but that kind of fight just wasn't in her. Besides, there was a chance that Nate could be right.

In some ways it would be better if he was.

After all, if Dent took the children, then he would keep them safe because he would use them to make a deal. Darcy was good at deals. And she would bargain with the devil himself if it meant getting her son back.

Nate didn't tack anything else on to his speculations about Dent, and the silence closed in around them. Except it wasn't just an ordinary silence. It was the calm before the storm because Darcy knew what was coming next.

"Charles Brennan," she tossed out there since she knew Nate had already thought of the man. Over a year ago Brennan had hired the triggerman who'd murdered Nate's wife.

"Yeah," Nate mumbled. "Any chance he's behind this?"

Well, Brennan was dead, but she didn't have to remind Nate of that. Because Nate had been the one to kill Brennan in a shoot-out after the man had taken a deputy hostage.

"Brennan made me executor of his estate," Darcy volunteered. "I've gone through his files and financials, and there is no proof he left any postmortem instructions that had anything to do with you. Or me, for that matter."

"You're sure?" Nate pressed.

"Yes." As sure as she could be, anyway, when it came to a monster like Brennan.

Nate made a sharp sound that clipped from his throat. It was the sound of pure disapproval. "Brennan was a cold-blooded killer, and you defended him."

She had. And two months ago she would have argued that it was her duty to provide representation, but that was before her client had nearly killed a deputy sheriff, Nate and heaven knows how many others.

Darcy kept watch out the window. She didn't want to look at Nate because she didn't want him to see the hurt that was in her eyes. "There's nothing you can say that will make me feel worse than I already do," she let him know.

Silence again from Nate, and Darcy risked touching him so she could lean in and see the mileage. Just under twenty miles to go. Still an eternity.

Nate's cell buzzed. "It's Kade," he said and flipped open the phone.

Just like that, both the dread and the hope grabbed her by the throat. She moved closer, until she was shoulder to shoulder with Nate. Darcy no longer cared about the touching risk. She had to know what Kade was saying.

"I'm on the side of the hill with a good binocular view of the Lost Appaloosa," Kade explained. "And I have good news and bad."

Oh, mercy. She wasn't sure she could handle it if something had happened to the children. Nate's deep breath let her know he felt the same.

"The good news—there's a black van parked on the side of the main house," Kade continued. "Something tells me this one isn't a decoy."

"How do you know?" Darcy asked before Nate could. She wanted to believe that was good news, but she wasn't sure. "Do you see the children?"

"No sign of the children," Kade told them. His voice was practically a whisper, but even the low volume couldn't conceal his concern.

Kade paused. "Nate, call Grayson and the others and tell them to get out here right away. Because the bad news is—there are at least a half-dozen armed guards surrounding the place."

Chapter Five

Nate parked the SUV near Kade's truck—a good quarter mile from the Lost Appaloosa ranch house.

This had to work.

He'd already set his phone to vibrate and had Darcy do the same. Now, he slid his gun from his shoulder holster, eased his SUV door shut and started down the exact path his brother had instructed him to take. A path that would hopefully keep them out of sight from those guards patrolling the place.

Nate glanced back at Darcy and put his index finger to his mouth, even though he had already made it clear that they had to make a silent approach. Not easy to do considering Darcy was wearing those blasted high heels. Still, she'd have to adjust. The last thing he wanted was to give anyone a reason to fire in case the babies were nearby.

Part of him prayed this wasn't another decoy—even though, according to Kade, the half dozen or more guards were armed to the hilt. At least if Noah and Kimmie were here, then Nate would finally know where the children were. Of course, that was just the first step.

He had to get them out—safe, sound and unharmed.

Even though it was late afternoon, it was still hot, and sweat began to trickle down his back. So did the fear. He'd never had this much at stake. Yes, he'd lost Ellie, but that had been different. His wife had been a cop, capable of defending herself in most situations.

Kimmie was his little girl.

Nate choked back the fear and followed the beaten-down path until he spotted Kade on the side of a grassy hill. His brother was on his stomach, head lifted so he could peer over the top. Kade also had his gun drawn.

Kade glanced at him, but his brother's eyes narrowed when he looked at Darcy.

Yeah.

Nate wasn't pleased about her being there, either, but he hadn't had a choice. If he'd left her at the sheriff's office, she would have just tried to follow them. And he couldn't have blamed her. If their situations had been reversed, he would have done the same.

"The others are on their way," Nate whispered. He dropped down next to Kade.

Darcy did the same, her left arm landing against Nate's right one. Close contact yet again. Contact Nate decided to ignore. Instead, he took Kade's binoculars and looked at their situation.

It wasn't good.

Nate didn't need but a glimpse to determine that. All the windows had newspaper taped to the glass. No way to see inside.

Outside was a different set of problems.

There were armed gunmen milling around the ranch house. All carried assault rifles and were dressed in black. Nate counted three, including the one standing guard at the front door, but then he saw one more when the man peered out from around the back of the house. There was yet another on the roof and one on the road near the cattle gate that closed off the property.

The gunmen had an ideal position because they controlled the only road that led to the ranch, and they obviously had good visibility with their comrade perched on the roof. Plus, there was a lot of open space around the ranch house itself. There were barns and a few other outbuildings that could be used for cover, but it wouldn't be easy to get to the house without being spotted by one of those armed goons.

"Are the children there?" Darcy whispered.

"Can't tell." Nate handed her the binoculars so Darcy could see for herself.

"Grayson and the others should be here soon," Nate relayed to Kade. "I called him just a few minutes before we got here, and he's bringing an infrared device so we can get an idea of who's inside."

And how many. That was critical information so they would know the full scope of what they were up against.

"How many will be with Grayson?" Kade asked.

Nate mentally made a count. Grayson, Dade, Mason and Mel. "Six total with you and me."

Even odds. Well, even odds for the gunmen outside the house, but Nate was betting there was some firepower inside, as well.

"The FBI should have a choke hold on the surrounding area in place in about an hour," Kade let him know.

A choke hold. In other words, the agents would be coming from the outside and moving in to make sure no one got away if the gunmen scattered. Nate was thankful for the extra help, but an hour was a lifetime.

Besides, he didn't want the gunmen spotting the agents and opening fire.

"This is San Antonio P.D.'s jurisdiction," Nate reminded his brother.

Kade nodded. "I want family calling the shots on this."

Yeah. Because for Nate and the rest of the Rylands, this was as personal as it got. Nate trusted the FBI, had worked well with them on many occasions, but he didn't want anyone thinking with their trigger fingers or their federal rules. But he also didn't want emotions to create a deadly scenario.

That included Darcy.

Beside him, her breath was still racing, and she had the binoculars pressed to her eyes. "How do we get in there?" she asked.

"*We* don't," Nate quickly corrected her. He took the binoculars from her and had another look. "You'll stay here."

"And what will you be doing?" she challenged.

That would be a complicated answer so he turned to Kade. "I need a closer look at the house. A different angle so I can try to see in one of the windows."

Kade gave him a flat look. "Grayson is bringing infrared," he reminded Nate.

Yes, but Nate didn't think he could just lie there waiting for his brother and the equipment to arrive. "I have to know if Kimmie is all right," he mouthed, hoping that Darcy wouldn't hear him and echo the same about Noah.

Kade huffed, glanced around and then grabbed the binoculars. "You stay here with Ms. Burkhart."

Nate caught his arm. "It's my daughter. I should take the risk."

No flat look this time. This one was cocky. "Won't be a risk if I do it," Kade assured him. "Stay put, big brother. My head is a lot more level than yours right now."

Nate couldn't argue with that, but man, he wanted to. He wanted just a glimpse of his baby to make sure she was okay.

Kade hooked the binoculars around his neck, shot a stay-put glance at them and began to crawl to the left side of the hill. He went about twenty feet, ducking behind some underbrush and then behind an oak.

Nate kept his eyes on Kade until he disappeared from sight, and he turned his attention back to the gunmen. He wouldn't be able to see as well without the binoculars, but at least he could detect any movement that might indicate if one of them had spotted Kade.

"They have to be all right," Darcy mumbled. She, too, had her attention nailed to the patrolling gunmen.

Nate heard the sniffle that she was trying to suppress. This was obviously ripping her apart, and he wanted to comfort her.

Okay, he didn't.

He didn't want to be pulled into this strange bond that was developing between them. He couldn't. But then Darcy sniffed again, and Nate saw the tear slide down her cheek.

Hell.

So much for cooling down this bond.

He couldn't slip his arm around her because he

wanted to keep his gun ready, but he did give her a nudge, causing her to look at him.

"I'm a good cop," he reminded her. "So are my brothers. We *will* get the children out of there."

Darcy blinked back fresh tears. Nodded. And squeezed her eyes shut a moment. She also eased her head against his shoulder. It wasn't a hug, but it might as well have been. Nate felt it go through him. A warmth that was both familiar and unfamiliar at the same time. He recognized the emotions, the comfort, that only a parent in Darcy's position could give.

But there was also some heat mixed with that warmth.

Even though she was still the enemy on some levels, she was also a woman. An attractive one. And his body wasn't going to let him forget that.

She opened her eyes, met his gaze. Until Nate turned his attention back where it belonged—on the gunmen.

"I could go out there," Darcy whispered. "I could offer myself in exchange for the children. Hear me out," she added when he opened his mouth to object. "If they kill me, then you'd still be here to save Kimmie and Noah."

"Admirable," Nate mumbled. "But stupid. We don't need a sacrificial lamb. We just need some equipment and a plan."

And apparently both had arrived.

He heard movement—footsteps—and Nate took aim in that direction just in case. But it wasn't necessary because he spotted Grayson, Dade, Mason and Mel inching their way through the grass toward them.

Nate eased away from Darcy, putting a little space between them, but it was too late. He knew from Grayson's slightly raised eyebrow that he'd taken note of the contact and was wondering what the devil was going on.

"Kade's trying to get a look inside the windows," Nate said, ignoring Grayson's raised eyebrow. He tipped his head in the direction where he'd last seen Kade.

"This should help." Grayson handed Nate the handheld infrared scanner, and all four crouched down on the hill next to Darcy and him.

Nate didn't waste any time. He put his gun aside, turned on the device and aimed it at the house. The human images formed as red blobs on the screen, and the first thing he saw was an adult figure.

And then two smaller ones.

"The babies," Darcy said on a rise of breath. She probably would have bolted off the hill if Nate hadn't latched on to her and pulled her back to the ground.

Yes, the smaller figures were almost certainly the children, and the person who appeared to be holding them was probably Marlene. Judging from the position of the blobs, Marlene was sitting with the babies on her lap. They were in a room at the back of the ranch.

Mason mumbled some profanity, and Nate didn't have to guess why. Marlene and the babies were alone in the room, but they weren't *alone*. There were two larger figures at the front part of the house. Men. And judging from the placement of their arms, they were holding weapons.

"At least eight of them," Nate supplied. That meant whoever was behind this had some big bucks and a very deep motive.

Dade took the infrared and aimed it at other out-buildings, no doubt to see if there were guards inside.

The movement to their left sent them all aiming their weapons in that direction, but it was only Kade.

"The windows of the house are all covered," he relayed to them. "But I do have some good news. No cameras or surveillance equipment that I can see mounted on the house or anywhere near it. Plus, four FBI agents are in place on the outside perimeter of the property, and more are on the way. The ones here are waiting for orders."

Grayson pulled in a long breath and looked at Nate. "We should wait here for another call from the kidnappers. It's clear they want something, and eventually they'll have to say what so we can negotiate release of the hostages."

It was standard procedure. The most logical option. And Grayson had spelled it out like the true cop he was.

"Wait?" Darcy challenged. Nate kept her anchored to the ground by grabbing her arm.

Grayson nodded. "I've already alerted the bank in case we need a large sum of cash, and every road leading away from the area is being watched."

"But our babies are in there," Darcy sobbed. She was close to hysterical now, and Nate knew he had to do something to keep both her and himself calm.

"I vote for having a closer look," Mason said. With just those few words, he had everyone's attention.

"We don't need a warrant because we've seen proof that the children are inside with armed kidnappers. That makes it an immediate-threat situation."

Nate couldn't argue with that.

"I brought a tranquilizer gun rigged with a silencer,

and I can get on the roof and take out the guard there. That would give us some breathing room. Plus, I'm wearing all black, just like them, so I can blend in."

Nate took that all in and saw an immediate problem. "The guy on the road—"

"Would have to be taken out, too," Kade supplied, finishing what Nate had started to say. "I can do that hand-to-hand. I can sneak up on him using those trees to the right. I'll knock him unconscious before he can take a shot and neutralize the threat." He looked back at Mason. "And how the devil do you plan on getting up on the roof?"

"Black van," Mason growled. "It's parked right by the side of the house."

It was, and if Mason could make it that far undetected, he might be able to crawl on top of the van and tranquilize the guard on the roof. The key to this kind of approach was to go in as quietly as possible.

"And then what?" Grayson pressed, staring at Mason.

Mason shrugged. "I'll see if I can quietly take out some of the others with the tranquilizer gun."

Grayson stayed silent a moment and then tapped the infrared screen. "Someone would have to be positioned to go in through the back to get to Marlene and the children while someone else is occupying the two in the front of the house—especially the one on the porch."

"I'll take the front," Dade volunteered. "Once Kade's finished playing hand-to-hand with the guy on the road, he'll be close enough to move in so he can help me out if I need it."

"That leaves the back of the house for me," Grayson spelled out.

"Or me," Nate piped up.

"Bad idea," Grayson let him know.

Kade echoed the same, and it was Kade who continued. "If you're down there and the kidnappers call, then you could get us all killed just trying to answer your phone."

"Best if Darcy and you wait here," Grayson finished.

Darcy looked at Nate and shook her head. "I have to do something to help."

Oh, this was going to be hard. Nate understood Darcy's need because it was his need, too, but Grayson was right. A call from the kidnappers could be deadly if Darcy and he were near the ranch house.

"We have to stay here," Nate told her. And like before, he got at face level with her so he could force eye contact. He kept his voice as calm and gentle as he could manage. "We'll be able to help. We can keep watch and alert them if anything changes or goes wrong."

There was no debate in her eyes. Just the inevitable surrender. "I'll watch the infrared," she finally said. Darcy took the device and focused on it.

Nate looked up at Grayson. "You'll need backup."

"Yeah. I'll have Mel positioned with a rifle somewhere down there." Grayson pointed to a heavily treed area that was still on high ground but much closer to the ranch than they were now.

"And then there's you," Grayson added. He handed Nate another rifle, which he'd taken from the equipment bag that Mel had with her.

His brother didn't mention that if Nate had to fire, it would be dire circumstances. But it would be.

"Kade, call your agents and tell them the plan. I want

them positioned and ready as backup." Grayson paused a moment. "And if anything goes wrong, then we all pull out. No shots are to be fired into the house." He glanced at each of them. "Questions?"

No one said a thing. Grayson gave Nate one last glance, and his brothers and Mel started to move. They were already out of sight before Nate admitted to himself that the plan could be a really bad idea. But staying put could, too. Without a working crystal ball, he had no idea what approach was best, but he did know he had to do everything to get the babies out of there.

The sooner, the better.

"It'll be okay, right?" Darcy asked without taking her attention from the infrared.

"It will be." Nate tried to sound as convinced as he wanted to be, and he put his handgun in his holster so he could get the rifle into position.

"I think they're sleeping," she added, staring at the screen. "And it looks as if Marlene is rocking them."

It did. The babies certainly weren't squirming around, but that made him wonder—had they been drugged?

That tore right at Nate, and he had to take a deep breath just to loosen the knot that put in his throat.

"Noah will want his dinner soon," Darcy whispered.

Nate knew where she was going with this, and he figured it had to stop. They would drive themselves mad considering all the things that could go wrong. He glanced at her. But stopped when he heard a sound.

A snap, as if someone had stepped on a twig.

Not to the side, where the others had walked. This sound came from behind them.

Nate turned, trying to get the rifle into position. But it was already too late.

The man stepped through the wall of thick shrubs, and aimed the gun right at Nate.

Chapter Six

From the corner of her eye, Darcy saw the alarm register on Nate's face.

She whirled around, praying it was one of Nate's siblings but no such luck. Dressed head to toe in black, the man also had black-and-dark-green camouflage paint smeared on his face. He had on some kind of headset with a marble-size transmitter positioned in front of his mouth.

But it was the gun that grabbed her attention.

It was big and equipped with a silencer similar to Mason's weapon.

Oh, mercy.

This was *not* part of the plan.

"Don't," the man warned when Nate tried to shift his rifle toward him. "If you want to live long enough to see your kids, then put the gun down. Slowly. No sudden moves."

Darcy hung on every word. She didn't want to do anything to cause him to fire. But she also studied what she could see of his face.

Did she know him?

It certainly wasn't Wesley Dent or anyone associated

with his case. In fact, she was reasonably sure she'd never seen this man before.

"Boss," the gunman said into the transmitter of his headset, "we got visitors. The kids' parents are up here in the woods. They got guns and infrared. They're looking at you right now."

Darcy glanced at the infrared screen and saw one of the men move from the front of the house to the back, where Marlene and the children were.

"Will do," the man said to his boss. He kept his cold, hard stare and his gun on Nate. "Stand up," he demanded. "We're going for a little walk."

That nearly took the rest of Darcy's breath away, but then it occurred to her, if he'd wanted them dead, he could have just shot them while he was in the bushes.

Nate started to move, but the man growled, "Wait!" in a rough whisper. His eyes narrowed, and he adjusted the transmitter portion of his headset. "Boss, there's a uniform with a rifle at your eight o'clock. About three hundred yards from where I'm standing. She's in firing range of the house."

Oh, no. He'd spotted Mel, and the deputy wasn't looking back at them. Mel had no idea she'd been detected.

Darcy couldn't hear what the person on the other end of the line was saying, but she figured it wasn't good.

"How many are here with you?" the gunman demanded, his attention still fixed on Nate.

"Just the three of us," Nate lied.

The gunman didn't respond to that, but his eyes narrowed. "Boss, I'll take out the uniform and then bring these two down for a chat."

Darcy watched in horror as the gunman took aim at

Mel. She reacted completely out of instinct. She drew back her foot and rammed the thin heel of her right shoe into his shin. Nate reacted, too. He dived at the man, slamming right into him, and they both went to the ground. So did the man's headset.

"Run!" Nate told her.

Darcy turned to do just that, but she stopped. Nate was literally in a life-and-death struggle with a much larger, hulking man, and she had to do something to help.

But what?

She glanced over her shoulder to see if Mel had noticed what was going on. The deputy hadn't. Darcy started to yell out a warning to her, but again she stopped. If she yelled, heaven knew how many gunmen she'd alert, and the men inside the house might try to get away with the children.

Or they might do something worse.

Besides, Mason and the others were probably close to approaching the house now, and if she sounded the alarm, it could get one of them killed.

Darcy looked around and spotted the rifle. She couldn't risk firing a shot, but maybe she could use it. She grabbed the barrel and tried to use the rifle butt to hit the gunman.

She failed.

Nate and the man were rolling around, their bodies locked in the struggle, and if she were to hit Nate accidentally, then it could cost them the fight. And this was a fight they couldn't lose.

"What's going on?" she heard someone ask over the headset.

Her heart dropped again. It wouldn't take long before

the person on the other end of that transmitter realized something was wrong, and that might cause the boss to take some drastic measures.

Nate must have realized that, as well, because she heard him curse, and he revved up his attempt to control the man's gun. Both had fierce grips on the weapon, and the gunman was trying to aim it at Nate.

Darcy kicked the guy again when she could reach his leg. And again. While Nate head-butted the man.

The sound somehow tore through the noise of the struggle.

It was a loud swish. As if someone had blown out a candle. But Darcy instinctively knew what it was. The gun had been fired, the sound of the bullet muffled through the silencer.

"Nate!" she managed to say.

Oh, mercy. Had he been hit?

She dropped to her knees and latched on to Nate's shoulder, to pull him away. There was blood. Lots of it. And a hoarse sob tore from her throat.

"I'm okay," Nate assured her. But he didn't say it aloud. He mouthed it so that no one on the other end of that transmitter could hear him.

But Darcy shook her head. He couldn't be okay, not with that much blood on the front of his shirt.

He repeated, "I'm okay." Again, it was mouthed, not spoken. And he scrambled off the gunman, who was now lying limp and lifeless on the ground.

Nate wrenched the gun from the man's hands and put his mouth right against Darcy's ear. "He pulled the trigger," he let her know. "And missed me. He hit himself instead."

Her sob was replaced by relief, and she threw her

arms around him. Nate was alive and unharmed. She couldn't say a prayer of thanks fast enough.

"We can't stay here," Nate insisted, his mouth still against her ear. He glanced at the headset next to the dead man.

Darcy nodded. He was right. They couldn't stay there because it wouldn't be long before someone came to check on him. Nate and she had to be long gone by then.

Nate kept the gun with the silencer in his right hand, and caught her arm with his left. He started to run, hauling her right along with him, and he headed in the direction that his brothers had taken.

Darcy's heart was already pounding from the fight, and her heels didn't make it easy to race over the uneven terrain. But she couldn't stop or give up. Not with her baby's life at stake.

She wanted to know where Nate was taking her, but she didn't dare ask. The woods were thick, without much sunlight here, and she didn't know if there were other armed guards hiding in the shadows, waiting to strike.

They ran, zigzagging their way through the trees and underbrush. No sign of his brother or Mel, even though Darcy thought they were heading in the deputy's direction.

Nate glanced down at his hip, and for one horrifying moment, she thought maybe he'd been hurt, after all. But she realized his phone was vibrating. He mumbled some profanity and ducked behind a tree.

"It's Grayson," he whispered. Nate didn't answer it. Instead, he fired off a text: Position compromised. Am on the run.

Nate shoved his phone back in his pocket and took her by the arm again. He jerked her forward as if ready to run but then stopped.

"Hell," he mumbled. His grip melted off her arm.

Nate lifted his hands in the air. Darcy did, too, though it took her a moment to realize what was going on. She finally saw the gun. Not a handgun, either, but some kind of assault rifle.

And, just like earlier, it was aimed right at them.

"DROP YOUR GUN," the man ordered Nate. "Take the other one from your holster and drop it, too."

Nate couldn't believe this. He still had blood on his hands from the last attack, and here he was looking down another gun barrel.

"Now!" the man snarled.

Nate glanced at Darcy, to let her know he regretted what he had to do, and he dropped the guns. First, the one he'd taken from the dead guard and then his own Glock.

"Start walking," the gunman demanded the moment the weapons were on the ground. He used the assault rifle to point the way.

This guy was even bigger than the other, and he kept several yards between them so it would be next to impossible for Nate to attack him.

"What do we do?" Darcy whispered. She stumbled, and Nate caught her arm to stop her from falling.

"We look for an opportunity to escape," he whispered back. But he knew that wouldn't be easy.

The guard was leading them straight to the ranch.

Darcy's suddenly rapid breathing let him know that she realized that, as well.

Nate kept walking and glanced around, hoping he'd see one of his brothers or Mel. But he saw no one, other than the guard who was patrolling the road. Once Darcy and he were out of the trees and into the open, the guard on the porch would spot them, as well.

But where were Mason and Kade?

They should have made it to this point now. Nate prayed nothing had gone wrong.

And then there was Mel to consider.

If she was still perched on the side of that hill, she might try to take out one or two of the guards when she saw that Darcy and he had been taken captive. That would mean bullets being fired much too close to the house. Nate knew Mel was a good cop with good aim, but he was uneasy enough with Mason's plan. Nate didn't want bullets added to this already dangerous mix.

Darcy stumbled again right as they reached the dirt road that separated the woods from the ranch. Again, Nate caught her.

"Should I pretend to faint or something?" she whispered.

"Keep moving!" the guard demanded, and this time he didn't whisper.

"Do as he says," Nate instructed. It appeared the guy had plans to take them inside the house.

When they stepped out onto the road, the guard moved closer to them. Probably to protect himself. Did he know Grayson and the others were out there? Maybe. Or maybe he was just being cautious.

The guard by the cattle gate came closer, as well, and he kept his rifle aimed at Darcy and Nate. The man fired glances all around, and his message was clear—if anyone took a shot at him, he would shoot back, and at this range, he wasn't likely to miss.

"They're taking us to the children," Darcy mumbled. She quickened her pace, hurrying across the yard and to the porch.

The door swung open, and the two guards forced them inside, following right behind them. They shut the door and immediately started watching out the gaps in the newspapers that covered the two front windows.

Other than a tattered sofa and some boxes, the room was empty, and Nate couldn't hear the babies or Marlene.

"Welcome," a bulky man said from the doorway of the kitchen. Like the others, he was dressed all in black and had camo paint on his face. And he was armed.

"Are you the boss?" Nate asked.

"Yeah," he readily admitted.

Nate tried to commit every detail of this man's appearance and demeanor because when this was over, the boss was going down.

"Where are the children?" Darcy demanded. Her voice was shaking. So was she. But she managed to sound as if she was ready to tear them limb from limb.

"I'll let you see for yourself." The boss stepped to the side and motioned for them to go toward the back of the house.

Was this some kind of trick?

Maybe.

Nate certainly didn't trust them, but several of the guards had had more than ample opportunity to kill them.

"This way," the boss instructed. He led them through a dining room and then to a hall.

That's when Nate saw the open door. And the room.

"Noah!" Darcy practically shoved the boss aside and hurried toward Marlene and the babies. They'd been right about the rocking chair. Marlene was seated in it with Kimmie in the crook of one arm and Noah in the other.

Marlene's eyes widened, but that was her only reaction. Maybe because she was in shock. No telling what these goons had put her through.

"Noah," Darcy repeated.

She scooped up her sleeping son into her arms. Nate did the same to Kimmie, but neither baby stayed asleep for long. Noah immediately started to fuss, and Kimmie slowly opened her eyes.

Nate felt the rush of panic as he tried to check his daughter to make sure she hadn't been hurt. She was still wearing her pink overalls, and there were no signs of bruises or trauma.

"Da Da," Kimmie babbled, and she smiled at him.

That nearly broke his heart and filled it in the same beat. His baby had been through so much—too much—and yet here she managed a smile. Nate didn't even attempt one. He just pulled Kimmie deep into his arms and held her as close as he could while he kept an eye on the goon standing behind them.

Beside him, Darcy was doing the same to Noah, and there were tears streaming down her face.

"I tried to stop them," Marlene said, shaking her head. She backed away from them as if she might try to bolt through the window.

"She did," the boss verified. "And she might have a few bruises because of it."

Nate had to stop his hands from clenching into fists.

He wanted to break this guy's neck for hurting Marlene and putting them through this nightmare. But he had to hold on to his composure. He would do battle with him, but it wouldn't happen now. First, he had to figure out how to get Kimmie, Noah, Marlene and Darcy out of there.

"Why did you do this?" Nate demanded. He tried to keep the rage out of his voice for Kimmie's sake.

The boss met Nate's glare. "I've been instructed to offer you and Ms. Burkhart a deal."

"What kind of deal?" Darcy snapped. Noah was still fussing so she began patting his back.

Nate waited for what seemed an eternity for the boss to respond, and the dangerous thoughts kept going through his head. All the things that could go wrong. His brothers might not know Darcy and he were inside, and if they didn't, they could be about to put their plan in motion.

A plan that might cause these SOBs to fire shots.

Nate brushed a kiss on Kimmie's forehead and prayed nothing would go wrong.

"It's a simple request." The boss didn't continue until he leaned against the doorjamb. What he didn't do was lower his gun. "You're to transfer two million into an offshore account."

This was about money?

Of course, Nate had considered it, but then why had they taken Noah? Darcy was doing okay financially, but he was pretty sure she wasn't rich.

"Two million?" Nate verified. He could transfer that amount with a phone call.

"Yeah," the boss said. "For starters. Part two of the deal is slightly more…complicated. You're to make sure

Wesley Dent is not only arrested for his wife's murder. He's also to be convicted."

Nate heard Darcy pull in her breath. He had a similar reaction, including disgust. Yeah, he thought that Dent might be guilty, but he wasn't a dirty cop, and he didn't fix investigations.

So, why did this bozo want him to fix this one?

His first guess was that these gunmen worked for either Sandra Dent's son, Adam, or her ex-husband, Edwin. Both had motives for wanting Dent behind bars.

Which meant Dent might be innocent, after all.

"Wesley Dent is my client," Darcy clarified. "I'm supposed to defend him to the best of my abilities."

"Admirable," the man snarled. "But being admirable won't get your son back."

"What do you mean by that?" Nate demanded.

"I mean we're holding your children until we have the results we want for Dent. If you want to speed things up, I suggest you get Dent to confess. Or create a confession for him."

"That can't happen." Nate turned, adjusting his position so that Kimmie wouldn't see the anger on his face. "And you can't keep our children for what could turn out to be months."

Another shrug. "Well, we can't keep them here, of course. We have to move them as soon as you leave." He checked his watch. "And your time is up. You have to go now."

"No!" Darcy tightened her grip on Noah.

"This could all be over by tomorrow," the boss calmly explained. "Talk Dent into confessing and then arrange for his suicide because he feels so guilty for killing his wife."

"No," Darcy repeated, and she looked at Nate and shook her head. "I can't leave Noah here."

Nate was about to assure her that they weren't leaving, but the sound stopped him cold. Not a shot.

But a thud.

The boss's expression changed immediately. He was no longer calm. "See what's wrong," he barked to the young gunman behind him. The boss reached out, latched on to Marlene's hair and pulled her in front of him.

And he put the gun to her head.

Hell.

They didn't need that. Nate had figured he could give Kimmie to Marlene so his hands would be free, but that option was out now. Instead, he handed her to Darcy, and he was thankful that his baby seemed to enjoy being in the arms of this stranger, who cuddled her as protectively as she was cuddling her own son.

"Don't do anything stupid," the boss warned Nate.

There was another sound. Not a thud. But the noise of a tranquilizer gun.

Mason.

His brother was out there. The Ryland plan was in motion.

Nate moved closer to Darcy and the babies, positioning himself between them and the gunman. It wasn't much, but it was the best he could do for now. He braced himself in case he had to lunge for the guy. What he didn't brace himself for was the crash that came through the window behind him.

Darcy tried to move away from the breaking glass. And the boss let go of Marlene. The man took aim at the window and probably would have fired, but Nate dived at him, knocking both the man and his weapon to the floor. His body was still stinging from the fight with the last guard, but he had adrenaline and need on his side. His baby's life was at stake.

"Mason?" Darcy called out. There was relief in her voice, which hopefully meant his brother hadn't been hurt.

Nate continued the struggle, trying to pin the boss to the ground. But the guy just wasn't giving up, and he was fighting hard.

"Stay back," he heard Mason say, and a moment later, his brother was there. The tranquilizer gun was in the waist of his pants, and he'd drawn his sidearm.

Mason reached into the scuffle, and he grabbed the boss by the throat. He dragged him away from Nate and put his gun directly under the man's chin.

"Move and I'll kill you now," Mason warned. "Less paperwork for me to do."

Nate thought that was a bluff. But then, maybe not.

"Get Darcy and the babies out of here," Mason told Nate. He hauled the boss to his feet and muscled him toward the front. "Marlene, too. And hurry."

Nate took Kimmie from Darcy. "Is the outside secured?" Because he didn't want to bring the children out of the house if the gunmen were still out there.

"Kade's people found some explosives," Mason informed him. "They disarmed the ones they found, but they might not have gotten them all."

"Explosives?" Darcy asked. There was no relief in her voice now.

"Yeah," Mason verified. "We must have tripped a master wire or something because they're all set to detonate in about five minutes. Get out of here *now*."

Chapter Seven

Run!

The word kept racing through Darcy's head as she, Nate and Marlene rushed out of the house with the babies cradled in their arms.

Mason was behind them, dragging the boss along, but Darcy concentrated only on her own steps. Running in high heels put her at a huge disadvantage, but she couldn't fall. Couldn't stop. Even though her lungs were already burning.

She had to get her baby away from a possible explosion.

"This way!" someone shouted.

It was Dade, and he was motioning for them to follow him onto the road. Beside him, on the ground, was one of the gunmen, and he was either unconscious or dead because he wasn't moving. There was no sign of Grayson or Kade.

Nate dropped behind her and used his free hand to latch on to her arm. Good thing, too. Because she stumbled, and if it hadn't been for Nate she would have fallen.

"I'm taking genius, here, this way," Mason let them know.

And he started in another direction through the

woods where Darcy had last seen Mel. Maybe because Mason didn't want the boss anywhere near the children. Darcy was thankful for that, but she also hoped the gunmen wouldn't attack again and help their boss escape.

The sound that came from behind them was deafening, a thick blast. Darcy just held her son closer and didn't look back, but it was clear that something had blown up. She prayed Nate's brothers, Mel and the FBI agent hadn't been hurt or killed.

Both Noah and Kimmie were crying now, and their sobs tore at her heart the way nothing else could.

Mercy, what they'd been put through.

And for what?

To rig the investigation so that her client would be arrested and convicted of his wife's murder. Once they were safely away from this place, Darcy wanted answers about who had orchestrated everything. No one was going to get away with endangering these children.

Dade led them back toward the start of the path, where they'd left the vehicles. It seemed to take forever, and each step was a challenge.

"Get in the SUV," Nate ordered, and he jerked open the door and shoved Darcy into the backseat. He pushed Kimmie into her arms and looked behind him.

"Where's Marlene?" Nate asked.

Dade, who was breathing hard, looked behind them, as well. He only shook his head and cursed.

Marlene was nowhere in sight. God, no. Had she fallen? Darcy certainly hadn't heard her, but then she hadn't been able to hear much over the roaring in her ears.

"Go ahead," Dade insisted. "Get them away from here. I'll look for her."

Nate didn't argue. He ripped the keys from his pocket, jumped into the driver's seat and started the engine. He gave Dade one last glance before he hit the accelerator and sped away.

Darcy held a crying baby in each arm, and she pulled them to her and tried to soothe them. "Shhh," she whispered, brushing kisses on each of their heads. "It's okay. Mommy and Daddy are here."

Kimmie looked up at her, the tears spilling down her cheeks, and she glanced at Nate, whose attention was fastened to the road. For a moment Darcy thought the little girl might sob again, but Kimmie rubbed her eyes, smearing the tears on her little hands, and she settled her head against Darcy's shoulder.

All right.

That required a deep breath. Darcy hadn't expected to feel this, well, attachment to Nate's daughter. But Kimmie felt as right in her arms as Noah did. Strange. It had to be a reaction to the fear.

Darcy didn't have time to think about it because there was another blast. It was so loud, so strong, that it shook the SUV.

"Hell," Nate mumbled.

Terrified of what she might see, she looked back and saw more of the nightmare that had started when she'd first learned someone had kidnapped her son.

The house was a fireball. The barn, too.

And so were the woods where she'd last seen Mason.

"Call me the minute you know anything," Nate said to Grayson.

Nate pushed the end-call button on his cell and released the breath he'd been holding. Finally, he had some good news to go with the not so good. Of course, the best news was in his arms.

Kimmie was asleep, her head resting right against his heart, and they were safely back at the Ryland ranch.

Nate had already said prayers of thanks, but he intended to add a lot more. Having Kimmie safe was the most important thing in his life, but his brothers were a close second.

He looked across the foyer and saw Kimmie's nanny, Grace Borden. The petite woman with graying red hair was studying his face. "Well?" she asked in a whisper.

"My brothers are okay," he relayed. Grayson had just let him know that. "And they found Marlene hiding in some bushes. She's shaken up but all right."

Grace nodded and walked to him. "Why don't you let me take Kimmie and put her in her crib for the night?"

Nate wanted to hold her. Heck, he didn't want to let go, but his baby would sleep much better in her own bed than in his arms. Besides, he had to check on Darcy and Noah. He didn't want to wake Kimmie doing that.

Grace eased Kimmie from his arms. "I'll take good care of her," she assured him. It wasn't necessary. Nate trusted her completely, but it still tugged at him to see his daughter being whisked away. It might be a lifetime or two before he started to forget that she'd been stolen from him.

Someone would pay for that.

He felt the anger boil inside him. A lethal mix, but he pushed that powder keg of emotion deep inside him. Soon, he would get the men responsible for what had happened.

Nate went to the bar in the living room and poured himself a shot of whiskey. He took it in one gulp, even though he preferred beer to the fireball of heat that slid down his throat. Still, he needed something to settle his nerves.

He made his way to the family room, where he'd left Darcy as soon as they'd gotten back from the Lost Appaloosa. He had to tell her that Bessie, the housekeeper, had fixed a room for Noah and her.

Before he even got there, he heard the voices coming from the family room. Not Darcy's voice. But Kayla Brennan's, Dade's fiancée, who had already moved into the ranch. Good. Maybe talking with Kayla had managed to calm Darcy down because Nate didn't want to tackle that job.

"Yes, that was an obstacle," Kayla said. "Dade's family hated me."

Nate groaned silently and stopped. This didn't sound like a calming-down kind of conversation. He peered around the corner and saw both women seated on the leather sofa. Darcy held a sleeping Noah in her lap. Kayla had her sleeping son in her arms.

"I was Charles Brennan's daughter-in-law," Kayla continued. "The man who ordered Nate's wife to be killed."

"But Dade and his brothers obviously got past that," Darcy pointed out.

Yeah. But it hadn't been easy. Just a short time ago, Kayla had been the enemy.

Much as Darcy was now.

And that gave Nate a jolt. A nasty feeling in the pit of his stomach.

"That's true." Kayla shrugged. "I fell in love with

Dade, and everything else fell into place. The Rylands and my son are my family now." Her gaze flew to the doorway, where he was standing. "Nate," she greeted. She stood, slowly. "You have news?"

"They're all okay," Nate said as quickly as he could. "Dade doesn't have a scratch on him, and he'll be home soon."

Kayla made a sound of relief and blinked back tears. "Thank you."

Darcy mumbled a thank-you under her breath, and she closed her eyes for a moment.

Kayla glanced down at her son. Then, at Darcy, before her gaze went back to Nate. "It's time I put Robbie to bed." There was an inflection in her voice, an implied *so you two can talk.*

Yeah, they needed to do that. And Darcy probably wasn't going to like what he had to say. Nate waited until Kayla was out of the room before he started what was essentially a briefing.

One with a bad twist.

"Are your brothers really okay?" she asked.

"They are. Kade has a few cuts and scratches because he was close to one of the blasts, but his injuries are minor." He took a deep breath and rested his hands on his hips. "And they found Marlene. She said she got separated from us when we were running, and she hid in some bushes."

"That's good." Darcy stared at him, waiting.

"Come on." Nate motioned for her to stand. It might be better to finish this if he didn't have to see her face. There was concern, and fear, written all over it. "Bessie made up a bed for you. Noah, too."

She stood, not easily. Her legs were wobbly, but Nate

didn't move to help her. He'd been doing too much of that lately. Instead, he led her out of the family room, across the foyer and into the hall that fed into the west wing of the house.

"Okay, what's wrong?" Darcy asked.

Well, the woman was perceptive. "Only one of the kidnappers survived. The boss, aka Willis Ramirez. And he's not talking. Plus, I'm not sure how long we can even hold him."

"What?" It wasn't a whisper, either. Noah jolted, and Darcy frantically started rocking him. She also stared at Nate. "The man kidnapped our children."

"Yes, but Mexico has an extradition order for him. He worked for one of the drug lords and gunned down six people, including a high-ranking police officer."

The color blanched from her face, and he got her moving again so she could put Noah down. She looked too shaky to be holding anything right now, especially a baby.

"How much time do we have to interrogate him?" Darcy wanted to know.

"Not much. A day or two at most. Grayson is with him now and will keep pressing until the federal marshals arrive and take custody."

Darcy shook her head, mumbled something. "Grayson has to get a confession. We have to find out who hired him to kidnap the children."

"We will," Nate promised.

He opened the door to the guest suite and took her through the sitting area and into the bedroom where Bessie had prepared the crib. Bessie had also left Darcy a loaner gown, a robe and some toiletries.

Darcy laid the baby down, kissed one cheek and then

the other. She lingered for several moments, and Nate didn't rush her. He understood her reluctance to leave her baby.

Finally, she stepped away, keeping her eyes on Noah until she was in the sitting room. She groaned softly and leaned against the wall. "I don't know how I made it through this day," she whispered.

Nate was right there with her on that. He'd faced down armed criminals before, had even been wounded in the line of duty. But only Ellie's death came close to this.

"Tomorrow I'll have someone drop by your house and get some things," he told her. "If you need anything specific, make a list."

The weariness didn't fade from her eyes, but they did widen a bit. "I'm not going home?"

"No." Nate thought about how to say it and decided to just toss the truth out there. "The danger isn't over. If Ramirez doesn't give up the person who hired him, then one way or another I'll have to find out who he is. That might take some time."

She didn't argue. Didn't look as if she had the strength to put up even a token resistance. "And in the meantime?"

"Noah and you will stay here." That was the logical solution. The ranch had a security system. Plus, there were at least a dozen ranch hands on the grounds at any given moment. It also didn't hurt that five lawmen lived there.

And four of those lawmen might be a problem.

"Your brothers?" she said, getting right to the heart of the matter.

"There'll be tension," he admitted. "But no one here

will turn you out. The kidnappers went after our children. They might try again."

She shivered, and closed her eyes. Did she see the same nightmarish images that he did? The gunmen, the children huddled on the floor of the preschool? The explosions that tore apart the Lost Appaloosa only minutes after they'd rescued Noah and Kimmie?

Her eyelids fluttered open, and she met his gaze. "If Ramirez doesn't talk, I think we know where your investigation starts. Sandra Dent's son, Adam, or her ex-husband, Edwin Frasier."

Yeah. That ball was already rolling. Mason was arranging for both men to be brought to Silver Creek for questioning. Too bad they couldn't find the dead woman's missing diary. Then maybe they would know who was behind this. Nate knew from accounts from Sandra's friends that the diary existed, but it hadn't turned up in any of the searches of her estate. Of course, her killer could have destroyed it, and with it any possible evidence.

"I can't rule out Dent himself," Nate added. "He could have orchestrated this to make himself look innocent." He braced himself for the lawyer to kick in.

But she only nodded. "About how much would it have cost to put this kidnapping together?"

"Three vans, seven men, weapons, explosives. We're probably looking at a minimum of a hundred thousand." He hesitated. "Unless Ramirez's drug-lord connections are behind this. Then the men could have been coerced into helping with the kidnapping."

A heavy sigh left her mouth, and she plowed her hands through her hair to push it away from her face.

But then she winced when her fingers raked over her stitches.

Nate moved her hand so he could have a look, which required him to push aside a few strands. Her hair was as soft as silk. And despite their ordeal in the woods, she didn't smell of sweat and blood but rather the faint aroma of the fragrant cedars. Her own scent was there, too. Something warm and musky.

Something that stirred feelings best left alone.

"Well?" she prompted.

"The stitches held." But there was an angry bruise around the edges. He made a mental note to call the doctor and ask him to come out to the ranch to examine Darcy. He also made a mental note not to let her scent get to him.

"How does it look?" she asked. But she waved him off. "Never mind. I know I look bad."

That was the problem. She didn't. Even with the fatigue, the stitches and the bruise, Darcy managed to look amazing.

Beautiful.

And that was not a good thing for him to notice.

Nor was her body. It was pretty amazing, too. She was a good eight inches shorter than he was. On the petite side. But she still had interesting curves. Curves that reminded him it'd been too long since he'd held a woman.

Or had one in his bed.

His own body responded to that reminder. His blood started to race. His heart, too. And his jeans were no longer comfortable.

Nate stepped back, or rather, tried, but she caught his arm. "I'm sorry."

Of all the things he'd expected her to say, that wasn't one of them.

He studied her eyes. Also beautiful. And he shook his head, not understanding her apology. He was the one with the bad reaction here.

"I'm sorry for everything," Darcy clarified. Her voice was mostly breath now. "Especially for defending the man whose hired gun killed your wife. I'm sorry I managed to keep him out of jail so that he could go after Dade and Kayla."

Oh, hell, no. Nate didn't want to go there. He didn't want to talk about Ellie. So he shook off her grip and turned to leave.

"For what it's worth," Darcy continued, "I've applied to be the assistant district attorney here in Silver Creek."

That froze him in his tracks, and Nate eased back around to stare at her. As the A.D.A, she'd have to work with Grayson, Dade and Mason. Work *closely* with them, on the same side of the law.

"I'm not a bad person." Her voice trembled again. So did her bottom lip, and her eyes began to water. "I just got wrapped up in doing…what I thought I needed to do. Old baggage," she added in a mumble. "Something you might know a little about."

Oh, yeah. His old baggage had baggage.

"When did yours start?" she asked.

Nate didn't have to think about that. He also didn't have to think about it to know this was a conversation he didn't want to have. But he answered her, anyway. "Twenty years ago when I was fifteen, my grandfather was murdered, and it was never solved."

"Yes. Sheriff Chet McLaurin. Kayla asked me about him."

Nate was sure he blinked. "Why would she ask you that?"

"She called me a few weeks ago and wanted to know if I'd come across a photo of your grandfather in any of Charles Brennan's things. She faxed me a copy of the picture and said it was taken on the day the new sheriff's office opened."

Now, he understood. Kayla had asked because Darcy was the executor for Brennan's will, and the picture was definitely in question. Kayla had seen a copy, and now the family wanted to know why a man like Brennan had held on to a photo seemingly unrelated to him.

"Did you find the picture in Brennan's things?" Nate asked.

Darcy shook her head. "I looked but didn't find anything. It might turn up, though, because I'm still going through his estate." She paused. "Is it important?"

"Could be. Maybe there's something in Brennan's files that will tell us who killed our grandfather."

"I see." And a moment later, she repeated it. "When this is over, I'll look again." Another pause. "His death is the reason you became a cop?"

"Yeah." And this was another wound Nate didn't want reopened tonight so he turned the tables on her. "What baggage made you become a defense attorney?"

A pained look flashed across her face, and Darcy opened her mouth. Closed it. And that pained look got significantly worse.

"It's okay," he quickly assured. "The conversation's over." And he was probably as thankful for that as she was.

They didn't need to be delving into baggage or what had brought them to this point. Didn't need to be discussing anything personal.

He especially didn't need to be thinking of her as an attractive, troubled woman he should haul off to his bed.

Besides, he had a mountain of stuff to do—stuff that didn't require getting Darcy naked and in his bed. Phone calls to make. An investigation to start. He also needed to see if Grayson had made any progress with Ramirez.

"If you need anything, my room is just across the hall," he let her know. "The security system is on, and all the ranch hands are on watch to make sure no one suspicious enters the property."

There. He'd doled out all the info she needed for the night, and he could go. Good thing, too, because he was exhausted.

But he didn't move.

His feet seemed glued to the floor.

Her eyes widened, as if she knew a fierce storm was already upon them. And it was. The storm inside him. Nate cursed. Because he saw the alarm on Darcy's face.

Followed by the heat.

Oh, man.

One-sided lust was bad enough, but two-sided was a disaster in the making.

His feet finally moved. In the wrong direction. Nate went to her, catching her hands and pinning them against the wall. Hell, he pinned her, too. Pressing his body against hers as he lowered his head.

And kissed her.

He captured her breath and the sound of her surprise

all at once. Nate might as well have had sex with her because the slam of pleasure was that intense. The instant awareness that he was about to lose it. And that taste.

Yeah.

Like something forbidden.

"Nate," she managed to say, the heat burning her voice.

He didn't attempt to say anything for fear that the sound of his voice would bring him back to his senses. For just this moment he wanted to be pulled deep into the fire.

He wanted to feel.

And he did. For those scalding-hot moments, Nate felt it all. The desire for a woman. The need to take her. The ache that he'd suppressed for way too long.

But he forced himself to remember that even with all those aches and burning needs, he shouldn't be kissing Darcy. Nate pushed himself away from her. Not easily. He had to force his body to move, and then he had to force it not to go right back after her again.

Their gazes collided.

In her eyes, he saw all that fire still raging. Heard it in her thin breath. Felt it pulsing in her wrist.

He let go of her, and her hands dropped to her sides. Nate watched her recover, hoping that he could do the same.

"What was that?" she asked, breathless.

"A mistake." He was breathless, too.

She stared at him, the pulse hammering in her throat. Since looking at her throat made him want to kiss her there, Nate took another step back. And another for good measure.

Her gaze slid over his face, his chest, which was pumping as though starved for air. In a way, it was. Then, her eyes lowered to the front of his jeans.

Where she no doubt—*no doubt*—saw the proof of just how much that kiss had aroused him.

"We can blame it on the adrenaline," she whispered.

For some reason, a stupid one, probably, that made him smile. For a split second, anyway. And then reality crashed down on his head. He shouldn't be kissing her and he shouldn't be smiling.

"Good night, Darcy," Nate told her.

"Wait. There's something bothering you. Something other than *that*," she clarified, her attention dropping to the front of his jeans again.

Oh, man. This brain connection they had was almost as bad as the fire she'd started in his body. Darcy was right—something was bothering him. He'd intended to keep it to himself. Because it could alarm her. But heck, he'd already opened a big box of alarm just by kissing her.

"Did you think there was anything strange about Ramirez when the gunman took us into the ranch house?" he asked.

She stayed quiet for a moment. "You mean stranger than the fact he had kidnapped our children?"

"Yeah. He didn't ask us how we'd found them."

"You're right." Darcy pulled in her breath. "Neither did the gunmen in the woods."

Nate made a sound of agreement. "They seemed ready for us. As if they'd been expecting us all along. But why would that be? The only reason we went to the Lost Appaloosa was because Marlene wrote the initials on the van door."

She pressed her fingers to her forehead. "And from what we know, Marlene might not have even been in that particular van. It could have been just a decoy."

"So who wrote the initials?" Nate finished for her. "And why did Ramirez want us to find him?"

"I don't know." She shook her head. "Do you?"

"No. But first thing in the morning, I intend to find out."

Chapter Eight

"I'm fine, really," Darcy told the Stetson-wearing doctor again, but Dr. Doug Mickelson continued to slide his penlight in front of her eyes. He'd already examined her stitches and a small cut she'd gotten on her elbow.

She wanted this exam to end so she could go back to her son. Darcy could feel the anxiety creeping through her, again, and she wondered how long it would take before she could get past the ordeal of the kidnapping.

Never was a distinct possibility.

"You're sure the children are okay?" Darcy asked when the doctor plugged the stethoscope into his ears so he could listen to her heart.

"They're right as rain," he assured her. "They were lucky."

Yes, and she hated that something as fragile as luck had played into keeping Noah and Kimmie safe.

"All done," the doctor finally said. He hooked the stethoscope around the collar of his cowboy-style light blue shirt. "No concussion, but I'll need to see you early next week so I can take out those stitches."

She nodded but couldn't think beyond the next hour, much less next week. Darcy hurried off the foot of the bed, then out of the guest room and into the hall, leaving the doctor as he was putting his gear back into his medical bag. She got to the nursery, where she'd left Noah with Kimmie and the nanny, Grace Borden.

But the nursery was empty.

Just like that, the panic grabbed her by the throat. *No!* Had her son been taken again? She knew that wasn't a logical conclusion, but her mind wasn't logical right now. The pain was still too fresh.

"Noah?" she called out. She didn't even wait for an answer before she shouted out his name again.

"In here," Nate answered.

Darcy practically rammed into the doctor coming out of the guest suite, but she followed the sound of Nate's voice. And the sound of laughter. She found him in the last room at the end of the hall. A massive sunwashed playroom. Bright. With lots of windows and shelves loaded to the brim with books and stuffed animals.

It took her a moment to pick through the toys and the brightly colored furniture, but she finally spotted Nate. Not in danger. Not trying to stop another kidnapping. He was on his hands and knees on the floor.

Both Kimmie and Noah were on his back.

And Nate was giving them a pseudo horsey ride. He was even making the neighing sounds while holding on to them.

Kimmie's auburn curls were bouncing all around her face. Noah was doing some bouncing, too. Clearly her brain had overreacted because the children were in no kind of danger.

"Grace is in the kitchen having some breakfast, and Bessie brought you some of that cinnamon tea you said you liked," Nate let her know, tipping his head toward the tray on a corner table. But he must have noticed her expression. "What's wrong?"

"Nothing," she managed to say. "I panicked when I couldn't find Noah."

"Sorry. I thought it would be okay to bring him down here while you were with Doc Mickelson." He reached behind him and gently moved the children off his back and to the thick play mat.

"It's okay." Her son had obviously been having fun, and her panic had ended that fun.

Well, sort of.

Even though Noah was no longer on Nate's back, her son giggled and crawled into Nate's lap the moment he sat up. Noah babbled something and threw his arms around Nate's neck for a hug.

"He's not usually this comfortable with strangers," Darcy remarked. To give her hands something to do, and to settle her nerves, she went to the table and poured herself a cup of tea.

Nate shrugged. Or rather, he tried to, but Kimmie toddled right into him and he had to catch her to keep her from falling. Noah giggled again. Kimmie did, too.

"I guess Noah knows I like kids," Nate remarked.

And he did. There was no mistaking that. Nate started a gentle wrestling game that ended up with both babies landing on him in a tumbled heap.

Now, Nate was the one to laugh.

The sound was rich, thick and totally male. It went through her much as his kiss had the night before, and suddenly the panic was gone. In its place was that spark. Okay, it was more of a jolt that touched every part of her body.

Every part.

His looks didn't help ease that jolt. Nate was drop-dead hot—that was a given—but this morning he was rumpled hot with his dark stubble, jeans and charcoal gray shirt. It was only partially buttoned, and she got a great look at the perfectly toned chest that he'd used to pin her against the wall for that kiss.

Suddenly, Darcy wanted to be pinned and kissed again.

"What?" Nate asked, snapping her attention back to him. "You're smiling. I've never seen you smile before." His gaze slid down her body. "And I've never seen you wear jeans."

She glanced down at her jeans and rose-colored top because for a moment she forgot she was wearing anything at all.

Get ahold of yourself.

"Someone picked up clothes from my house for Noah and me," she told him, but he obviously already knew that.

"Kade," he supplied. "He also brought your cosmetics and meds that he found in your bathroom."

Oh.

Meds, as in birth-control pills.

She almost blurted out that the pills were to control her periods and not because she was having sex, but that seemed way too personal to tell Nate.

"I'll make sure to thank Kade. And all your brothers. Bessie and Grace, too." She added some milk to the tea so she could cool it down for a quick drink. "Your family really pitched in when we needed them."

"They always do," Nate mumbled, and it sounded like a personal confession that he hadn't intended to reveal to her.

Darcy understood. Other than Noah, she hadn't had any family for a very long time, and she missed the closeness. The blind acceptance.

The love.

And that was a personal confession she wasn't ready to make, either.

Since it seemed the wrestling play might go on for a while, Darcy finished her tea, put the cup aside and sank down on the floor next to them. Nate didn't look at her. He kept his attention on the children.

"Do I need to apologize?" he asked.

For a moment Darcy had no idea what he meant, but then Nate glanced at her. And she knew. This was about that scalding-hot kiss. "No apology needed. We just got caught up in the moment."

And that moment was still causing some heat to flow through her body.

"Yeah." He sounded as if he wanted to believe that. Did that mean he was still thinking about the effects of that kiss, too?

Darcy decided it was a good time to change the subject, especially since they had plenty of non-kissing things to discuss. "Any news about Ramirez?"

Nate shook his head. "He's still not talking, and the extradition is moving at lightning speed."

So, time was ticking away. Darcy hoped the man would spill something before he was flown back to Mexico.

"Grayson's bringing in both Adam and Edwin for questioning." He glanced at the cartoon clock on the wall. "He'll let us know when they arrive."

Good. Sandra Dent's son and ex-husband were keys to unraveling all of this. Darcy just hoped she could hang on to her temper and composure if one of them confessed to taking the children.

"The rangers have their CSIs at the Lost Appaloosa. Or rather, what's left of it. The explosions destroyed a lot of potential evidence." Nate paused. Definitely no smile or laughter now, though he continued to play with the children. "Two of the gunmen have been identi-fied, and they both belonged to a drug cartel linked to Ramirez. One of them is Ramirez's kid brother."

"His brother?" she questioned.

"Yeah, his name was David Ramirez. He was just nineteen, and he was the one I got in a wrestling match in the woods. The one I shot." Another pause. "We be-lieve the brother and all the gunmen belonged to the cartel because they each had a coiled rattlesnake tattoo on their left shoulders. That's the cartel's symbol."

That erased the warm, jolting memories of the kiss and chilled her to the bone. Drug dealers had kidnapped her son. The doctor had been right—they were lucky. Things could have gotten a lot worse than they had.

"It's okay," she heard Nate say. And she felt his hand on her arm. Touching her. Rubbing gently with his fin-gertips. Darcy figured she must have looked on the verge of fainting or something for him to do that.

"I've run financial reports on Adam and Edwin Frasier," he explained. His voice wasn't exactly all cop now. Or maybe that was her interpretation because he was still touching her. "Both father and son have the ready cash to set up an operation like the kidnapping."

"But why would they have risked something like this?" she asked.

"More money, maybe. Sandra Dent died without a will. That means her husband will inherit everything."

"Unless he's convicted of her murder," Darcy supplied. "Then Adam would inherit everything. And that makes him the top suspect."

"Yes, it does. But it's possible Adam and his father worked out this deal together. Or if Edwin is working alone, he could have figured it'd be easier to continue to get an allowance from his son than Dent. As it stands now, Edwin is paid an allowance for managing Sandra's charity foundations. You can bet if Dent inherits everything, he'll cut off Edwin without a penny."

Yes. But Darcy was having a hard time wrapping her mind around anyone risking children's lives for money. Even the fifty million dollars that was in Sandra Dent's estate.

She jumped when she heard a sudden sound in the doorway. It was Mason. With his shoulder propped against the frame, he was holding a cup of coffee and had his attention fastened to Nate's hand, which was still touching her.

Darcy quickly got to her feet.

She didn't want to cause trouble between Nate and his brothers, and judging from Mason's semi-glare, he didn't approve of her or little arm rubs.

"Ma Ma Ma," Kimmie babbled, and with her wispy curls haloing around her face, she toddled toward her dark, brooding uncle.

Mason put his cup on a shelf and scooped her up. "We gotta work on that vocabulary, curly locks. It's Uncle Mason, not Ma Ma."

Kimmie smiled a big toothy smile, dropped a kiss on his cheek and babbled some more. "Ma Ma Ma."

"Don't give her any candy," Nate warned when both

Kimmie and Mason started to reach in his denim shirt pocket.

·"Later," Mason whispered to the little girl. He placed his hand over hers. "When Daddy's not watching. I'll leave one for your pint-size boyfriend, too."

Darcy was more than a little surprised that this particular Ryland also had a way with children. Mason always made her want to take a step back, and until now she'd never suspected there was a fatherly bone in his body. Noah, however, didn't move. He stayed right by Nate.

"A problem?" Nate asked his brother. He stayed on the floor and accepted some plastic blocks that Noah began to dump in his lap.

"Not with the investigation. A ranching situation. Another cutter quit this morning."

"Again?" Nate mumbled something indistinguishable under his breath. He was clearly upset, and this conversation was a reminder that the Rylands had more going on in their lives than law enforcement.

"Yeah," Mason snarled. "What can I say? I'm not into arm touching to keep folks happy."

Mason had noticed, after all. She felt herself blush.

"What's a cutter?" Darcy asked to fill in the very uncomfortable silence that followed. "I was born and raised a city girl," she clarified when Mason gave her a flat look.

"A person who trains cutting horses. They're used to cull out or cut individual livestock from a herd," Mason finally explained. "But folks use them for competitions and shows."

"People pay a lot of money for a well-trained cutting horse," Nate went on. "And despite going through a trainer every six months, Mason produces some of the best cutting horses in the state."

If Mason was flattered by that, he didn't show it. Instead, he gave Kimmie one of those flat looks. "You impressed, curly locks? Didn't think so."

Mason kissed Kimmie on top of her head and set her back on the floor. "Cause some trouble today, okay?" He eased two foil-wrapped pieces of candy on the shelf, grabbed his coffee cup and strolled away.

"Bye-bye." Kimmie added a backward wave and then reached up toward the shelf where she'd no doubt seen her uncle leave the candy.

"Later, baby," Nate insisted.

But Kimmie didn't give up. The little girl went to Darcy, caught her hand and babbled something.

"Maybe I can distract her," Darcy said, smiling, and she lifted Kimmie into her arms.

Kimmie waggled her fingers in the direction of the shelf with the candy, but Darcy took her in the opposite direction. To another shelf.

One Darcy hadn't noticed when she walked into the room.

There were more pictures here. Dozens of them, all in gleaming silver frames. Some were candid shots of Nate and his brothers, including one Ryland she'd never seen. That had to be his late brother, Gage, who resembled Mason except he had a cocky grin. There was also a copy of the picture of Nate's grandfather, the one that Kayla had faxed her.

"I called my assistant this morning," Darcy told Nate, "and asked her to look into the matter of your grandfather's photo. If Charles Brennan had something to do with Chet McLaurin, then we might find it in his files."

Files that she and her assistant had total access to. If she could give Nate and his family this information, then she would. Of course, Darcy hoped it wouldn't be another round of bad news because her former client, Brennan, was now dead, but when alive he'd no doubt committed murder and a litany of other crimes.

"There's Daddy." Darcy pointed to one of Nate holding Kimmie. Behind them were several horses.

"Da Da Da," Kimmie babbled, and then she switched to "Ma Ma."

Darcy expected to see a photo of Mason, but it wasn't. She recognized the beautiful smiling woman from articles in the newspaper. This was Nate's late wife, Ellie, and she was wearing a wedding dress.

"Ma Ma," Kimmie repeated, and she clapped her hands.

"Ellie died when Kimmie was six weeks old," Nate said softly. "I thought the picture might help her know who her mother is."

Well, it was obviously working because Kimmie was reaching for the photo now and had forgotten all about the candy. Darcy carefully lifted the picture from the shelf and brought it closer to Kimmie.

"Ma Ma." And the little girl kissed it. Darcy saw then that there were dozens of smudges on the glass. No doubt from Kimmie's kisses.

It put a lump in Darcy's throat, and she eased the picture back onto the shelf. She saw it then. The little silver disk. When Kimmie reached for it, Darcy picked it up so the little girl couldn't get to it. She didn't want to risk Kimmie choking on it.

"A concho," Nate provided.

Darcy turned it over and saw the double *R*s on the back. "For your ranch?"

"Yeah." And that was all he said for several seconds. His mood darkened a bit. "My father gave me and each of my five brothers a concho. A family keepsake, he said. And then a few weeks later, he walked out and never came back."

She turned, stared at him. "What happened?"

But judging from the pain that went through his eyes, she was sorry she'd asked. "I'm not sure why he left. My mother wasn't sure, either, and his leaving destroyed her. She killed herself, and in her suicide note she begged Grayson to keep the family together." Nate lifted his shoulder. "And he did. End of story."

No. Not the end. The pain was still too raw for that. It didn't help with that lump in her throat, and it gave her added respect for the Ryland brothers. They'd raised themselves, kept their family together, and they'd done that under the worst of circumstances.

"Do you hate your father for abandoning you?" Darcy asked, holding her breath.

"Yeah. All of us do. Well, except for Kade. He was only ten when our father walked out." Nate tipped his head to the concho. "Mason put a bullet through his. Dade threw his away."

"But you kept yours," she pointed out. And he'd polished it. Or someone had. Because it had a gleaming shine.

"Only so I could remember how much it hurts when people do irresponsible, selfish things." He shook his head. "I don't want to be anything like my father because I would never put Kimmie through that. *Never.*"

It was the answer she'd feared. "Noah's father, Jake Denton, abandoned him. Jake's never seen Noah and swore he never would." And Darcy could see firsthand the pain that abandonment could cause.

Would Noah have the same bitterness that Nate had?

Darcy hated Jake for that. Hated that Noah would have this wound.

"It's my fault, of course," she added. "I should have chosen a better partner." Even though her pregnancy had been an accident. One she certainly didn't regret.

"Sometimes, even when you choose the right partner, it's not enough," Nate said. She followed his gaze, and he was staring at Ellie's picture.

Kimmie looked at her dad. Then, at Darcy, and even though she was just a baby, she seemed to realize something wasn't right. Kimmie hooked her arms around Darcy's neck and kissed her cheek.

Darcy smiled in spite of the sad moment.

Children were indeed magical, and Nate's daughter was no exception. Noah, however, disagreed. He must have objected to Darcy giving this little girl so much attention because he toddled toward them and tugged on her jeans. Darcy treated herself to holding both of them, even though they were a double armful.

She glanced at Nate, who was smiling again. After the hellish day they'd had, this seemed like a moment to savor.

What would it be like to have moments like this all the time?

Darcy hadn't let herself consider a relationship, not after Jake had burned her so badly. But what would it be like to be with Nate? Thinking about that caused the heat to trickle through her body again.

Nate made a *hmm* sound.

Did he know what she was thinking? Probably not. But that didn't erase the little fantasy in her head.

Then Nate's phone buzzed, and the moment vanished. Darcy snapped back to reality. Especially when she heard Nate greet the caller.

"Grayson," he answered. "You have news?"

She stepped closer, watching Nate's face.

"What?" Nate asked several second later, and he paused. Darcy couldn't hear anything his brother was saying, but Nate finally snapped his phone shut.

"Edwin and Adam Frasier just arrived at the sheriff's office," Nate relayed to her after dragging in a long breath. He was the cop again. All business. And he got to his feet.

"What's wrong?" she asked, afraid to hear the answer.

Nate looked her straight in the eyes. "Edwin and Adam both claim Dent and *you* were behind the kidnapping plot, and they say they can prove it."

Chapter Nine

Darcy wasn't denying anything that Edwin and Adam Frasier had claimed. In fact, she hadn't said more than two words on the drive from the ranch to the sheriff's office. She just sat in the passenger's side of his SUV and stared out the window.

That caused Nate to do some mental cursing.

He didn't need this now. He needed clear answers that would lead him to the person responsible for kidnapping Kimmie and Noah, and with this latest allegation, Nate was afraid these interviews wouldn't give him anything useful.

The moment Nate parked the SUV, Darcy got out, and she didn't wait for him. She stormed toward the back entrance, threw open the door and hurried inside.

"Where are they?" Darcy asked Mel, and the deputy hitched her thumb toward the interview room at the front of the building.

"Grayson's in there with them now," Mel let her know. "How are the kiddos?"

"Fine," Darcy mumbled. "Kade and Mason are staying with them while I straighten out this mess."

Okay. She clearly wasn't pleased, and Nate couldn't blame her since they'd accused her of being involved with the kidnapping. Still, he hoped she wouldn't try to attack one of them. He'd faced Darcy in court and legal hearings and had never once seen her lose her composure. But now her fuse seemed short and already lit. Just in case her temper was about to explode, Nate hurried to catch up with her.

She marched into the room and shot past Grayson, who was standing. Edwin and Adam were seated, and Darcy planted her fists on the metal table that separated them. She leaned in and got right in their faces.

"Explain to me what *proof* you think you have that would implicate me in this crime," she demanded.

The men exchanged glances but didn't exactly seem unnerved. Nate decided to do something about that. He, too, moved closer.

"Ms. Burkhart asked you a question," Nate clarified. He shut the door, locked it, pretended to turn off the interview camera and then slid his hand over his gun in his shoulder holster.

That got their eyes widening.

Nate knew both men. Had interviewed them extensively about Sandra's death. Edwin was fifty-three and looked pampered and polished in his blue suit. To the best of Nate's knowledge, the man had never had a job in his life, even though he did get an allowance for managing one of his late wife's charity foundations.

Adam was a younger version of his father. There were no threads of gray in his brown hair. No tiny lines around his blue eyes. But there was no mistaking he was his father's son. Like his father, he also lived off an allowance from his mother's estate.

"You're going to shoot us?" Edwin challenged, eyeing the stance Nate had taken with his gun.

"Depends," Nate tossed back. Normally, he didn't play cop games, but he was almost as pissed off as Darcy was. "Right now, I consider you two my top suspects. I think one or both of you is responsible for endangering my daughter and Ms. Burkhart's son."

Nate adjusted his position and leaned in so that Darcy and he were shoulder to shoulder. "And I'm also thinking you're both dangerous enough to try to run out of here now that you know you're suspects. If you do that, I'll stop you."

Adam practically snapped to attention, but the threat didn't seem to faze Edwin. Except for the slight stirring in his jaw muscles. Because Nate had interviewed him and because he'd cataloged the man's responses, Nate was guessing that Edwin was also riled to the core. The man was just better at hiding his emotions than his son.

"Why would you say I had a part in this?" Darcy demanded again.

Edwin lifted his shoulder, but it was Adam who answered. "Because you stole seventy-five thousand dollars from my mother."

Darcy looked at Nate and shook her head. "When, where and how did this supposedly happen?" Nate asked.

"A week ago at my mother's estate," Adam continued. "The money was taken from a safe while Darcy was in the house."

Darcy huffed. "I was there," she admitted. "With two San Antonio police officers who work for Nate. I wanted to see where Sandra had died in case it came up at the trial. But I didn't go anywhere near a safe, and I didn't take any money."

"Well, it was there before you arrived, and it wasn't

there after you left." Adam folded his arms over his chest. "We think you used the money to orchestrate this kidnapping."

"And why would I do that?" Darcy spaced out each word and glared at Adam.

"Simple. This makes your client look innocent. He's not. But the truth doesn't matter to you. The only thing that matters to you is winning and letting a killer like Dent go free."

Since that seemed to eat away at what little fuse Darcy had left, Nate took over. "You have any proof she took it? Security surveillance tapes? Eyewitnesses?"

"No." Edwin didn't glare. He just looked smug. "But who else would have done it? Adam did an inventory of that safe just minutes before she arrived, and when he checked the safe again later that afternoon, the cash was gone. Are you saying your own officers are thieves?"

"No." Nate could play the smug game, too. "I'm saying you two are troublemakers or liars. Maybe both. You honestly think Darcy would have done anything to endanger her son or my daughter?"

Darcy made a slight sound. Relief, maybe? Nate glanced at her and realized that's exactly what it was. Oh, man. Had she really thought he might believe she'd put her child in danger to clear a client?

But Nate took a mental step back.

Yesterday, he might have indeed believed it. Before he'd seen her reaction to Noah's kidnapping. Before he'd witnessed firsthand how terrified she was.

Before he'd kissed her.

Yeah, that was playing into this, as well.

The sweltering attraction. But Nate knew in this situation that the kiss wasn't clouding his judgment. Darcy hadn't taken that money, and she hadn't had anything to do with kidnapping the babies.

Grayson moved to the end of the table and sat down. He studied Edwin and Adam for a moment. "So, you're suggesting a lawyer with no criminal record would do something like this?" He didn't wait for them to respond. "Because she's not a suspect, and you two are."

"I did nothing wrong!" Adam shouted.

"Nor did I." Edwin's voice was almost calm. *Almost.*

"That remains to be seen," Nate let them know.

Edwin got to his feet. "Are you arresting us? Because this was just supposed to be an opportunity for us to tell you about her stealing that money and trying to clear her client. And I don't appreciate your intimidation tactics. If I'd known we would be grilled like this, I would have brought my attorney."

"Come on," Grayson fired back. "Did you really think you could walk in here and put this kind of spin on what happened? If Darcy had wanted to clear her client, she would have gone about it differently. Not using reverse psychology."

"And if she had criminal intent, she could have created and paid for a witness," Nate explained. "One that would have given Dent an airtight alibi. It would have been far cheaper. Far safer. And it wouldn't have put her baby's life on the line."

Nate leaned in so he could look them in the eyes. "But you two have a lot to gain if you put Dent behind bars. Or better yet, get him the death penalty."

"Dent made his own bed," Edwin insisted. "He's running scared because he's guilty. And he knows you can prove it. You've said so yourself that you believe he's guilty."

Nate had said that. He couldn't deny it. And maybe Dent was behind the kidnapping, but Darcy certainly wasn't. So, that meant either these two had been duped into thinking Darcy was guilty, or they were the ones trying to do the duping.

Edwin gave his suit an adjustment that it in no way needed. "We're done here. We've given you the information, and now we'll go to your captain at SAPD. We'll press him to file charges against…" He cut his eyes toward Darcy. And smiled an oily smile. "Well, whatever she is to you."

Nate didn't consider himself someone who had a bad temper, but Edwin's suggestion sent anger boiling through him.

"Who said we're done?" Nate fired back.

Surprise showed in Edwin's eyes. Adam seemed alarmed.

Grayson stood, gave Nate a nod. "I'll take things from here." He looked at the two men. "You have the right to remain silent—"

"You're arresting us?" Edwin howled.

"Detaining you for questioning and possible arrest for multiple felonies," Grayson clarified. "When you're done hearing your rights, I suggest you call a lawyer."

The two men started to protest, but Grayson glanced at Nate, and he knew what that glance meant. This was now an official interrogation. Not an interview. And that meant Darcy and he shouldn't be there.

"We can wait in Grayson's office," Nate said to her.

She looked ready to argue, and her gaze flew to Grayson as if he might allow her to stay. But Grayson only shook his head.

"Come on." Nate caught her arm and led her out of the room.

"Thank you," she whispered. "For sticking up for me in there."

He maneuvered her inside Grayson's office but didn't shut the door. Privacy and Darcy weren't a good idea, especially since her nerves were raw and right at the surface.

"It was a no-brainer. As I said, you love Noah too much to put him in danger."

Darcy looked at him and shook her head as if she didn't know how to respond to that. But she did respond. Man, did she. She stepped forward until she was pressed against him, and slipped her arms around him.

"I'm wired to handle stress," she whispered. "But not this kind."

Was she talking about Noah now, or this suddenly close contact between them? Nate wasn't sure, but that didn't stop him from pulling her into a hug.

Unfortunately, a hug he needed as much as she did.

He, too, was wired to handle stress, but it was different when his entire world was tipping on its axis. For so long he'd been living in a dark cloud of grief and pain over losing Ellie that he had nearly forgotten what it was like to feel something, well, good.

His body was burning for Darcy. There was no denying that. But that didn't make things easy. Or even acceptable. Wanting Darcy could put a wedge between him and his family.

Without breaking the armlock they had on each other, she eased back a little and looked up at him. A soft breath left her mouth. Like a flutter. And her face flushed with what he thought might be heated attraction.

Nate tested that theory by brushing his mouth over hers.

Yeah, attraction.

"We shouldn't act on this," Darcy whispered.

But she didn't back away. She kept her mouth hovering just beneath his. Her breath smelled like the cinnamon tea she'd had earlier, and he wanted to see if she tasted as good as she smelled.

But Nate didn't get the chance. The sound of the footsteps stopped him.

He braced himself for a face-to-face with one of his brothers, who would almost certainly notice all the heavy breaths and lust-filled eyes that Darcy and he had for each other. But it wasn't his brother.

It was Wesley Dent.

Nate stepped into the hall, directly in front of the man.

They knew each other, of course. Nate had interviewed and interrogated him at least a half-dozen times. Times that Dent apparently hadn't liked because his green eyes narrowed when he looked at Nate.

Unlike Edwin and Adam, there wasn't much polish here. Dent wore his usual jeans and untucked white button-down shirt that was fashionably rumpled. It was the same for his shoulder-length, highlighted, brown hair. As a rule, Nate didn't trust a man who got highlights and manicures. He especially didn't trust Dent.

Was he looking at the person behind the kidnapping?

Just the thought of it caused the anger to boil up inside him again.

"I heard about your daughter. And your son," Dent

said, glancing at Darcy before he brought his attention back to Nate. "You've arrested Edwin and Adam?"

"Not at the moment," Nate informed him. "They're here for questioning."

Dent's eyes narrowed again. "Why not just arrest them? They're behind this."

"Where's the proof?" Nate challenged.

"The motive is proof." Dent looked up, huffed, as if he couldn't believe Nate hadn't done the obvious— arrest his dead wife's ex and son. "Those two morons wanted you to set me up. To fix the investigation. If that isn't proof, I don't know what is."

"Maybe," Nate mumbled and he left it at that.

"How did you know about the kidnapping being tied to you?" Darcy asked. She stepped out into the hall with them.

Dent wearily shook his head. "It's all over the news. I tried to call your office, to make sure you and your son were okay, but your secretary said you were out indefinitely."

All over the news.

Though he hadn't turned on the TV or opened a newspaper, Nate didn't doubt that word had gotten out. Heck, this was probably a national story by now, especially with so many deaths and the kidnapping from a small-town preschool. But he did have to wonder how many of the details had been leaked. Details like the possible identity of the person who'd hired Ramirez to force Darcy and Nate into throwing the investigation.

"So, when will you be back at work?" Dent asked Darcy. "We need to discuss what's happened. *Alone,*" he added, sparing Nate a glance.

That was reasonable. After all, Darcy was his attorney, but Dent's remark stirred up other feelings inside Nate. Old wounds about Darcy and he being on opposite sides. And new wounds about his confused feelings for her.

"I'm not sure when I'll be back," Darcy let him know. She looked over her shoulder when the bell on the front door jangled.

Nate looked, too. After what had happened, he didn't feel completely safe even in the sheriff's office. He couldn't see who had arrived because Tina Fox, the dispatcher, stood to greet the person and blocked Nate's view. He did relax a little, though, because it was obvious Tina wasn't alarmed.

"Look, I know you've been through a lot," Dent complained to Darcy, "but my life is at stake. If the cops arrest me—"

"Mr. Dent, effective immediately I'm resigning as your lawyer," Darcy interrupted.

Both Nate and Dent stared at her, and Nate didn't know which of them was more surprised.

"I wouldn't be able to give my full attention to your defense," she continued. Her voice wavered a little but not her composure. "My secretary or assistant can give you other recommendations."

"I don't want another lawyer," Dent howled. "Good grief, the police are trying to pin my wife's murder on me. I need you to make sure that doesn't happen."

"I'm sorry." She shook her head. "But I simply can't represent you." She turned to go back into Grayson's office, but Dent stepped in front of her.

"You can't do this," Dent insisted. "I won't let you do it." He flung his hand toward Nate. "Is it because of him? Because he's turned you against me? Well, you're stupid to believe Nate Ryland. He's had it in for me since the moment Sandra drew her last breath."

Enough was enough. Nate stepped between Darcy and the man. "Dent, my advice is to make some calls. Find another attorney. Because you're probably going to want one with you when Sheriff Ryland questions you."

"Sheriff Ryland?" he said like profanity. "If any of you badge-wearing cowboys want to question me, then you get a warrant for my arrest because I'm done playing games." He aimed a glare at Darcy. "I'll settle things with you later."

Nate latched on to Dent's shirt and snapped the man toward him. "Is that a threat?"

Dent opened his mouth as if he might verify that, but he must have decided it would be a bad idea. He tore away from Nate's grip, cursed and turned, heading for the door.

Nate followed him, to make sure he did leave. Grayson would indeed want to question him, but that probably wasn't a good idea with Edwin, Adam and Darcy there. Besides, Dent needed a new attorney. Later, Nate would talk to Darcy about that, to make sure she was doing this for all the right reasons—whatever those reasons were.

For now, he watched.

Dent was moving at lightning speed. Until he reached the dispatcher's desk. And then he stopped and stared at the person on the other side of Tina.

That got Nate moving. Darcy, too. Nate wasn't sure who had captured Dent's attention, and he was more than a little surprised that it was Marlene. She had a bandage on her cheek, another on her arm, but she looked as if she'd physically weathered the kidnapping ordeal. Not mentally, though. The woman was practically cowering.

"Grayson said I needed to sign some papers," Marlene said, her head lowered, her bottom lip trembling.

"Papers?" Dent challenged, and his booming voice caused Marlene to look even more rattled. "Please don't tell me this woman had something to do with the kidnapping."

Nate put his hands on his hips and tried to figure out what the heck was going on.

"The gunmen took me hostage," Marlene explained. "I work at the Silver Creek Preschool and Day Care."

Dent stared at her. And then he laughed. "Oh, this is *good.*"

That got Marlene's gaze off the floor. "I didn't do anything wrong," she insisted. And then she turned the pleading gaze on Nate and Darcy. "I swear."

"What do you mean?" Nate demanded. When Marlene didn't answer, Nate looked at Dent.

But the man just smiled and headed for the door. "Why don't you ask her? Or better yet, ask Edwin. I'm sure he'd like to tell you all about it."

Chapter Ten

Darcy kept watch out the SUV window while Nate drove back to the ranch.

Even though she didn't think anyone was following them, she wanted to make sure. With the eerie turn in the investigation, Darcy didn't want to take any chances with their safety. Or the babies'. She certainly didn't want a second wave of kidnappers trying to follow them to the ranch.

Nate was keeping watch, too, but he also had his cell phone clipped to the dash. Ready. And waiting for a call from Grayson that would hopefully explain why her former client had suggested Marlene was associated with Edwin. Grayson hadn't quite dismissed the semi-accusation, but he'd insisted that Nate and she head back to the ranch and leave him to handle the questions, not just for Edwin but for Marlene.

That was probably a good idea because the anger was already starting to roar through Darcy. Not just for Marlene's possible involvement but because she'd seen firsthand the venom inside Dent. She'd thought he was innocent, but she wasn't so sure of that now. Plus, there was the money taken from Sandra's safe. Dent could have stolen it and used it to fund the kidnapping.

Of course, the same could be said for Edwin or Adam.

"In all the interviews I did regarding Sandra Dent, Marlene's name never came up," Nate commented.

"Same here." But what had come up was the tyrannical way that Sandra had treated others—especially her husband, her ex and her son. It was that behavior, and her net worth, that had provided the possible motive for her murder.

Nate took the final turn to the ranch, and finally his cell rang. And Darcy saw that it was Grayson's name on the caller ID. Nate jabbed the button to answer and pressed the speaker function.

"Well?" Nate immediately asked.

Grayson huffed. "Edwin and Marlene know each other."

That kicked Darcy's pulse up a notch. "How?" Nate and she asked in unison.

"In the worst way possible for our investigation." Grayson sounded tired, frustrated and riled. "They had an affair."

"An affair?" Darcy challenged. "Those two don't exactly run in the same social circles."

"No," Grayson agreed. "But they apparently met at a bar in San Antonio. He bought her a drink, and things went from there."

Nate cursed, and it mirrored exactly how Darcy felt. "Any idea if Marlene had something to do with the kidnapping?" Nate pressed.

"She says no. So does Edwin. He puts the blame directly on Dent."

Of course, he would. Dent was putting the blame

on Edwin and Adam, and the finger-pointing was just going in circles.

"Edwin says the affair was short, just a few weeks, and that it ended months ago," Grayson continued. "Marlene echoed the same, but I got to tell you, I'm not sure I believe her. After all, she had an entire day to give me a heads-up about her relationship with Edwin, and she didn't even mention it. I have to ask myself why."

Darcy's pulse went up more than a notch. "Are you holding her?"

"No. I told her not to leave town, that I would have more questions for her once I did some checking. I'll get her phone records and go from there. Edwin's, too. If they put this kidnapping together, I'll find a way to prove it."

"Thanks," Nate told him.

"There's more," Grayson said before Nate could hang up. "The two deputy marshals are here to extradite Ramirez."

"Already?" Nate cursed. And Darcy didn't blame him. They'd hoped to have more time to get Ramirez to talk.

"Yeah. And the marshals want to leave immediately. I can't stop them from taking him," Grayson explained. "But I'll try."

Nate thanked his brother again, hit the end-call button and stopped the SUV in front of the ranch house. But he didn't get out. Neither did Darcy. They sat there trying to absorb what they'd just learned. A woman they had thought they could trust, a woman they had believed had helped them by writing those initials, could be the very person who had helped put their children in grave danger.

Darcy stared up at the iron-gray sky for a moment. Everything suddenly felt heavy. Dreary, even. Probably because a storm was moving in. Literally. But that storm was inside her, too.

They got out of the SUV, and Darcy glanced around at the lack of other vehicles in the driveway. Good. Fewer brothers to face. When they went inside, she could smell Bessie's lunch preparations, but none of the others were around. However, there were several notes on the table, which Nate stopped to read.

"Where is everyone?" she asked, automatically making her way to Nate's wing of the house. Maybe it was the news about Marlene, but she had to see her son and make sure everything was okay, and she headed in that direction.

Nate was right behind her. "According to the notes, Mason is in his office in the ranch hands' quarters. Kayla and Grayson's wife, Eve, are in San Antonio. Eve had a doctor's appointment."

Alarmed, Darcy stopped and whirled around to face him. "Is that safe? I mean, the person behind the kidnapping might go after members of your family."

He shook his head and ran his hand down her arm. "It's okay. Kade's with them. Grayson considered having Eve reschedule the appointment, but because of her age, her doctor here wanted her to see a specialist in the city. It's just a routine checkup."

"Routine," Darcy repeated under her breath. An impending birth that the family should be celebrating, but instead they were under this cloud of fear. Well, she was, anyway. Darcy didn't think she could forgive herself if something happened to another member of Nate's family.

"Come on." His gentle touch morphed into a grip and he led her in the direction of Kimmie's nursery.

There were no sounds. That was a cause for more alarm until Darcy realized both children were in the nursery. Sharing Kimmie's crib. And they were both asleep. Grace, the nanny, was seated in a rocking chair, a paperback in her hand, and she put her finger to her lips in a *shhh* gesture and joined them in the hall.

"They were both tuckered out," Grace whispered. "Fell asleep after their snacks so I decided to let them have a little nap."

Noah didn't normally take a morning nap, but Darcy figured he'd earned one because of the ordeal and the disruption in his routine.

"We'll be in my office," Nate whispered to the nanny. "Buzz me when they wake up."

Nate took Darcy toward the end of the wing until they reached his office. Like the rest of the rooms, it was large. There was a sitting area with a massive stone fireplace, several windows, but the remaining walls were filled with floor-to-ceiling bookshelves.

"I like to read," he commented when she stood in the doorway with her gaze shifting from one section of the shelves to the other.

Judging from the sheer number of books, that was an understatement, and it made her wonder when he found time to do that. Or exercise. But his toned body certainly indicated that he worked out, and the treadmill in the corner looked well used. It was the same for the desk, which was topped with all kinds of office equipment.

Including a red phone.

"Are you a secret agent or something?" she joked.

The corner of his mouth lifted. "It's a secure line. I need it sometimes if I'm here in Silver Creek and some sensitive SAPD business pops up."

She figured that was often. Nate was a lieutenant, an important man in SAPD. "It must be hard to live this far away from your headquarters."

"Sometimes. But it'd be harder if I didn't have my family around to help." Nate took two bottles of water from the fridge behind his desk and handed her one. His fingers brushed hers.

A totally innocent touch.

But like all of Nate's touches, it had a scalding effect on her.

And Nate noticed. "Sorry," he mumbled.

She tried to shrug it off and get her mind onto other subjects. It wasn't easy, but thankfully there were many things in the room—not just Nate—to distract her.

There were the monitors, for instance. A trio of flat screens had been built into the wall. They were all on, and she recognized the playroom and the nursery where the babies were sleeping. The third, however, was an exterior shot of a lush green pasture dotted with horses.

"A way for me to keep watch on the ranch," he explained.

Nate typed something on his computer keyboard, and the pasture scene switched to one of the outbuildings. She saw Mason talking with one of the ranch hands.

"We all pitch in to do what we can to run the ranch, but Mason has the bulk of the workload on his shoulders." There was regret in his voice. And fatigue.

Darcy strolled to the fireplace to study the photos on the mantel. As in the playroom, there was a picture of his murdered grandfather.

Nate's old baggage.

Funny that his old baggage was intertwined with some of her unfinished business. She took a sip of water, turned to him. "As the executor of Charles Brennan's estate, I can give you keys and access codes for all of his properties, including his safety-deposit boxes. If my assistant doesn't come up with anything, you might be able to find something that connects him to your late grandfather."

Nate blinked. "You'd do that?"

"Of course," Darcy said without hesitation.

But she was aware that just two days ago she would have done more than hesitate. She would have refused, citing her client's right to privacy, but her views weren't so black-and-white now. Being around Nate and having her life turned upside down had given her some shades of gray to consider. And since Charles Brennan had been a cold-blooded killer, she felt no obligation to hide his sins from the world.

Or from Nate and his family.

"Thank you," Nate said, his voice just above a whisper.

She shrugged and stared at the family pictures. "I know something about family love. And pain," she added. "About how complex relationships can be."

He studied her. "Are you talking about yourself now?"

Darcy smiled before she could stop herself. "Maybe. A little." But the smiled faded. "I'm responsible for my father's murder."

It was the first time she'd said that aloud, but mercy, it was always there. In her thoughts, dreams. Nightmares.

Always.

Nate put his water bottle on his desk, shoved his hands in his jeans pockets and walked closer. "You think you're responsible?" he challenged. "From what I remember, your father went after the eighteen-year-old thug who attacked you when you were sixteen."

She whirled around, her eyes already narrowing. "How do you know that?"

He slowly blew out his breath. "I always do background checks on the lawyers I come up against in court."

It felt like a huge violation of her privacy. And it was. But then she remembered she'd done the same thing to Nate and any other cop she might be grilling on the witness stand.

"Know your enemy," she mumbled. She lowered her head. "I hate that you learned that about me. I keep professing I'm a good person—"

"You are." And that was all he said for several seconds. "Why would you think you're responsible for his death?"

The pain from the memories was instant. Fresh and raw. It always would be. "Because I shouldn't have been out with Matt Sanders to begin with. My dad had forbidden me from dating him because he believed Matt was a rich bully. He was," Darcy admitted. "But I didn't learn that until it was too late." Her gaze flew back to his. "Please tell me you didn't see the pictures."

But his silence and suddenly sympathetic eyes let her know that he had. Pictures of the assault. Black eyes. A broken nose. Busted lip. Along with assorted cuts and bruises. All delivered to her face by Matt after Darcy had gotten cold feet about having sex with him.

"If someone had done that to Kimmie, I would have gone after him, too," Nate confessed.

"Maybe."

He took his hands from his pockets, touched her chin with his fingertips, lifting it so that it forced eye contact. "Your father made a mistake by carrying a gun to confront your attacker, but you did nothing wrong."

That was debatable. A debate she'd had often and lost. "My mother blamed me. Even on her deathbed." Dying from breast cancer hadn't stopped her from giving Darcy one last jab of guilt.

"Your mother was wrong, too." He sounded so sincere. So right. But Darcy couldn't feel that rightness inside her.

Her father had shot and killed Matt Sanders. And because they hadn't had the money for a good lawyer, the public defender had done a lousy job, and her father had been given a life sentence. Which hadn't turned out to be that long since less than a year later, he'd been killed while trying to break up a fight in prison.

"Your father is the reason you became a lawyer," Nate stated, as if he'd read her mind—again. His voice soothed her. A surprise. Nothing had ever been able to soothe her when it came to the subject of her father. "One day, maybe we'll both be able to remember the good without the bad mixed in."

Darcy wished that for both of them. Especially Nate. And that hit her almost as hard as learning that he knew all about her past. She'd known that her feelings for Nate were changing. She blamed the danger and the attraction for that change of heart. But she was more than surprised to realize that she cared about his healing.

About him.

And that went beyond the danger and the attraction.

Oh, mercy.

She was in huge trouble here.

The corner of Nate's mouth hitched. As if once more he knew what she was thinking. Maybe he did.

"I'm about to make a big mistake," he warned her. "Stop me?"

Right. She had less willpower than he did.

"Not a chance."

Nate frowned now. Cursed himself. Then cursed her.

Clearly he was not pleased that neither of them was going to do anything about this. He leaned in. Closer. Until she felt his warm breath brush against her lips. She also felt the pulse in his fingers that were still touching her chin.

And she felt his body.

Because he closed the distance between them by easing against her.

It flashed through her mind that while they shouldn't be playing with fire, it felt right. As if they should be doing this. And more. Then, he put his mouth on hers, and Darcy had no more thoughts. No more mind flashes.

The fiery heat took over.

It was as if they were starved for each other because Darcy wound her arms around him when he yanked her to him. They fought for position, both trying to get closer, but that was almost impossible.

Darcy's burning body offered her a quick solution for that.

Get naked and land in bed. Or in this case, the sofa, since it was only a few feet away.

But Nate didn't take her to the sofa. He turned her, anchoring her against his desk while he kissed the breath right out of her. His mouth was so clever, just the right pressure to make her beg for more. And then he gave her more by deepening the kiss.

The taste of him made those flames soar.

But it wasn't just the kiss. He touched her, too. First her face. Then her neck. Using just his fingertips, he traced the line to her heart. To her left breast. And to her nipple. It was puckered from arousal, and he used those agile fingers to work some heated magic there.

Darcy would have gasped with pleasure if her mouth hadn't otherwise been occupied by his.

She hoisted herself onto the desk so she was sitting. Behind her, things tumbled over, and she heard the sound of paper rattling. But that didn't matter. The only thing that mattered now was feeding this fire that Nate had started. So, she wrapped her legs around him and urged him closer.

Until his sex was against hers.

Yes, she thought to herself. This was what she needed, and judging from the deep growl that rumbled from Nate's throat, he needed it, too.

The kiss got even more frantic. It was the same for the touching. Each of them was searching for more, and Nate did something about that. He eased her down, so that her back was on his desk, and he followed on top of her. The contact was perfect. Well, except for their clothes, and Darcy reached to unbutton his shirt.

But Nate stopped her by snagging her wrist.

He looked her straight in the eyes. "This is just stirring up trouble," he mumbled. "I'm sorry for that."

For a moment, a really bad moment, Darcy thought he was about to call the whole thing off. But Nate shoved up her top and pulled down her bra. He put his mouth to her breasts and kissed her.

Okay, this was the opposite of stopping. She reached for his shirt again. However, Nate let her know that he was calling the shots because he got on the desk with her, pinning her in place with his body.

They were going to have sex, she decided. Right here, right now. And while she tried to think of the problems that would cause—and it would cause problems—she couldn't wrap her mind around anything logical.

Especially when Nate unzipped her jeans.

And slid his hand into her panties.

His first touch was like a jolt, and Darcy might have jolted right off the desk if he hadn't continued to pin her down. He kept up those maddening kisses to her breast and neck while he touched her in the most intimate way. It was making her crazy. Making it impossible to speak. Or move. Or do anything except lie there and take what his hand and mouth were dishing out.

Darcy felt herself racing toward a climax and tried to pull back so that Nate and she could finish this together. She wanted more. She wanted sex. But she was powerless to stop what Nate had already set in motion.

His fingers slid through the slick heat that his touch had created, and he didn't stop. Not with the touching. Not with the kissing. But what sent her over the edge was what he whispered in her ear.

"Let go for me, Darcy."

And she did. Darcy shattered, her body closing around his fingers as his mouth claimed hers. He kissed her through the shattering and deep into the aftermath.

Until reality hit her squarely between the eyes.

Mercy.

What the heck had she just done?

"Yeah," Nate mumbled. It was that "I'm right there with you" tone. "Trust me, though, it would have been, um, harder if we'd had sex."

Because Nate was indeed hard—she knew because of the way they were still pressed together. Darcy couldn't help herself. She laughed.

Nate's eyebrow rose, and he smiled. "I thought there'd be regret."

Oh, there was some of that. Nate was probably regretting it'd happened at all, and Darcy was regretting they hadn't just taken it to the next level.

"Hand sex crossed just as many lines as the real thing," she let him know. "Plus, it was only pleasurable for me."

He leaned in. Kissed her hard. "Don't think for one minute that you were the only one who enjoyed that."

And it seemed like an invitation for more. Darcy's body was still humming, but one look at Nate and she was ready for him all over again.

"It'll have to wait," he insisted.

For a moment Darcy thought the buzzing sound was all in her head, but then Nate let go of her. That's when she realized the sound was coming from his desk.

He pulled in several hard breaths as he made his way to the phone. Not the red one but the other landline. Nate snatched it up.

While she got off the desk and fixed her clothes, she

looked up at the monitors. The babies were still asleep, thank goodness. But her sense of relief faded when she saw the look on Nate's face.

"Where?" he demanded of the caller.

Nate cursed and punched some buttons beneath the monitor of the pasture and zoomed in on the high chain-link fence. Darcy saw nothing at first, but then the movement caught her eye.

There.

Someone was scaling the fence. Dressed in dark clothes with a baseball cap shadowing the face, the person dropped to the ground.

And that someone was armed.

"STAY PUT AND LOCK DOWN the house. I'm going out there to confront this SOB," Mason insisted.

"Be careful." Nate knew it was an unnecessary warning. Mason was always careful, and his brother would no doubt take a ranch hand or two with him. But the sight of a gunman meant plenty of things could go wrong.

Or maybe they already had.

Had Ramirez's boss hired someone else to come after them? Was this the start of another kidnapping attempt?

Nate hung up, and while he kept his attention on the monitors, he pressed in the code that would set the alarm for every door and window of the main house. He also took the gun from his desk drawer.

Beside him, Darcy was trembling now. She had her fingers pressed to her mouth. Her eyes were wide with concern and fixed on the screen with the intruder. An opposite reaction from what she'd had just minutes earlier.

Later, Nate would figure out why he'd had such a bad lapse in judgment by taking her that way on his desk. But for now, they had a possible kidnapper on the grounds.

"Please, not again," Darcy whispered.

Nate knew exactly how she felt. He didn't want the children, Darcy or anyone else to be in danger again. And in this case the danger didn't make sense. The person behind this had already failed to get Darcy and him to throw the investigation. Heck, Darcy was no longer even Dent's attorney.

But maybe this guy didn't know that.

"I need to go to the children," she insisted and headed for the door.

"No. Stay here. For now we just need to keep watch, to make sure Mason can handle this. There are no viewing monitors in the nursery, and it'll only upset the kids if you wake them from their naps."

Nate tapped the screen where the nursery and the babies were displayed on the monitor and hoped she would keep her focus there.

She didn't.

Darcy volleyed glances between the babies and the menacing figure making his way across the back pasture. Nate zoomed in on the intruder, trying to get a better look, but the baseball cap obstructed the man's face. Still, Nate had a sense of his size—about six-two and around one-eighty.

"How far is he from the house?" Darcy's voice was trembling, too.

"A good three miles. That part of the property is

near the county road." And that was probably why he was there. It wouldn't have been difficult to drive off the road and onto one of the old trails. Then hide a vehicle in the thick woods that surrounded the ranch. And maybe the intruder hadn't realized that any movement on the fence would trigger the security system.

"He's moving fast," Darcy observed.

Yes. He was practically jogging. While he kept a firm grip on his gun. A Glock, from the looks of it. There was something familiar about the way the man was holding it.

And that created an uneasy feeling inside Nate.

He flipped open his phone and called Grayson. "Tell me Ramirez is still behind bars."

Grayson didn't answer for a second or two, and that was an answer in itself. "Dade and Mel are on their way out there right now. It's possible Ramirez escaped."

Nate cursed. "He did. And he just scaled the west fence and is headed toward the ranch. How the hell did that happen?"

"Still trying to work that out, but neither of the marshals is responding."

Probably because they were dead. Nate didn't want to believe the marshals were in on this, that they'd let Ramirez escape, but later he'd have to consider it. If so, Ramirez's boss not only had deep pockets, he had connections.

"Dade is calling Mason now to tell him," Grayson explained.

Good. At least then Mason would know what he was up against. "How soon before Dade and Mel arrive?"

"Ten minutes."

That wouldn't be soon enough because once they

arrived, they would still have to make it out to the pasture. There was no way Mel and Dade would get there in time to give Mason immediate backup.

"I've tapped into the security feed," Grayson went on. "I can see everything that's happening, and I'll alert Mason if the gunman changes directions." With that, he hung up.

Nate could only curse again and watch the monitor. Yeah. It was Ramirez all right. But why come after them here? Why continue a plan that had already failed?

Those questions created an unsettling possibility.

"Ramirez will spend the rest of his life in jail if he's extradited," Darcy pointed out. "And his life might not be worth much since he killed a police officer. He must know he could die a violent death in prison." She paused. "This could be a suicide mission."

Oh, yeah. Death by cop. But Nate kept that agreement to himself.

He gave the security cameras another adjustment and located Mason. His brother was armed, of course, and was on horseback. One of the ranch hands was indeed with him, and they were both riding hard. It wouldn't take them long to close the distance between Ramirez and them.

When Nate went back to Ramirez, he saw that the man was now talking on a phone. Unless it was a prepaid cell, maybe they could trace the person he was calling. Nate opened his phone to request that trace, but he stopped cold.

"What's Ramirez doing?" Darcy asked. She moved closer to the screen.

Nate wasn't sure. Well, not sure of anything but the

obvious, and that was Ramirez had quit jogging. He rammed the cell into his pocket, turned and broke into a run—heading back toward the fence.

"He's leaving." There wasn't just fear in Darcy's voice. There was alarm.

Nate was right there with her. Even though it would put Mason in some danger, he wanted this situation to end now. He wanted Ramirez captured. Or dead. He didn't want him melting back into those woods so he could regroup and come after Darcy and the children again.

He turned to Darcy, knowing she wasn't going to like this, but also knowing there was no other choice.

"Go to the children," Nate ordered. "Lock the nursery door and don't come out until I give you the all clear."

She snapped toward him and grabbed his arm. "What are you doing?"

"I'm stopping Ramirez." Nate brushed a kiss on her cheek, shook off her grip and ran as fast as he could.

Chapter Eleven

Things were moving so fast that Darcy had trouble catching her breath.

She raced to the nursery as Nate had insisted and locked the door. She braced herself to explain everything to Grace, the nanny, but the woman was on the phone. Judging from her pale face and frantic tone, she was already aware of the danger. Thankfully, though, the children weren't.

Both Kimmie and Noah were still sound asleep.

"We're leaving," Grace said the moment she got off the phone. "When Dade and Mel get here, they're taking us to the sheriff's office. We're supposed to meet them at the front door." The woman hurried to the crib to scoop up Kimmie.

Darcy shook her head. "But what about Nate and Mason?" She didn't want to leave until she was certain they were safe.

"Grayson's orders," Grace explained. "He's worried that Ramirez could double back and get close enough to the house to shoot through the windows."

Darcy's heart nearly stopped.

She hadn't even considered the attack could escalate like that. Yes, she was still terrified for Nate and Mason, but she had to put the babies first.

Darcy grabbed a diaper bag, picked up Noah, who immediately started to fuss, and followed Grace out of the room, through the hall and foyer, and to the door. The timing was perfect because Dade and Mel pulled to a screeching stop directly in front of the steps.

"Hurry!" Dade insisted.

It was starting to drizzle, and Darcy tried to shield Noah with the diaper bag.

With his phone sandwiched between his shoulder and his ear, Dade continued to talk with someone. Grayson, she quickly realized. Dade rushed them into the backseat of the SUV, and Mel sped away. There were no infant seats so Darcy and Grace kept the babies in their laps.

Darcy wiped the rain from Noah's face, then Kimmie's, and looked out at the endless pasture, but she couldn't see Nate anywhere. That only caused her heart to pound harder. Not good. She felt on the verge of a panic attack, even though she knew it couldn't happen. Dade didn't have time to coddle her now, not while two of his brothers were in immediate danger.

"What if Nate and Mason need backup?" Darcy asked.

"They're cops," Dade reminded her. "Plus, the ranch hands are there." He sounded confident about that, but she noticed the hard grip he had on his gun, and his attention was glued on the pasture.

Soon, though, the pasture and the ranch were out of sight, and Mel sped down the country road toward town. Grace had her hands full trying to comfort a crying Kimmie. Noah was still crying, too. But Darcy tried to hear the phone conversation Dade was having with Grayson. She did. And heard something she didn't want to hear.

"The marshals are dead?" Dade asked. "Both of them?"

Oh, mercy.

She knew which marshals he meant—the ones who'd been escorting Ramirez. And now Nate was out there with a monster who'd killed before and wouldn't hesitate to kill again.

"Are you okay?" Grace whispered to her. Probably because the nanny had noticed that Darcy was trembling from head to toe.

"Everything will be all right," Darcy answered, and she repeated it, praying it was true.

Mel didn't waste any time getting them to the sheriff's office, and she pulled into the parking lot, angling the SUV so they were at the back entrance. Both Dade and Mel helped them into the building, and Dade locked the door before he rushed ahead of them to Grayson's office.

Grace stayed back a little, maybe so she could try to calm Kimmie, but since Noah's cries were now just whimpers, Darcy went with Dade in the hopes that she'd be able to hear news about Nate and Mason.

But Grayson stepped into the hall first. One look at his face, and Darcy knew something was wrong. "Is it Nate?" she asked, holding her breath.

"He's okay." Grayson's attention went to Dade. "But Ramirez got away."

That robbed her of her breath. This couldn't happen. This nightmare had to end. "Nate's out there. Ramirez could come after him."

Grayson shook his head. "Nate's already on his way back here."

Darcy was thankful for that, but she knew until he stepped inside the sheriff's building that he was essentially out there with a killer.

Dade started to curse, but he bit off the profanity when he glanced at Noah. "How did Ramirez escape?" Dade demanded, taking the question right out of her mouth.

Grayson shook his head again. "He made it back to the fence before Mason could get to him, and he disappeared. We'll keep looking," Grayson said first to Dade and then to her.

Darcy didn't doubt they would look, and look hard, but as long as Ramirez was a free man, then Nate, the children and she were all in danger.

"We're bringing in the rangers to assist in the search," Grayson explained. "The FBI, too."

"What do we do with them?" Dade hitched his thumb to Noah and her.

Grayson scrubbed his hand over his face and leaned closer to his brother so he could whisper. "Take them upstairs to the apartment. For now." He looked past Darcy and into the room behind her. "While we're waiting for news, I'll start this interview."

Darcy turned and saw Adam seated at the gray metal table. She turned to Grayson for an explanation as to why Adam was still there, but the young man got up and went to the door. However, he didn't focus on Grayson but rather Darcy.

"I didn't know," Adam said. "I swear."

"Didn't know what?" Darcy asked. And her mind began to whirl with all sorts of bad answers. She wasn't sure she could stop herself from going after Adam if he was about to confess to having some part in Ramirez's escape and the murder of those federal officers.

"About my father's affair with Marlene." Adam's forehead was bunched up. "He never said a word to me about it, and now I have to wonder—what else is he keeping secret?"

Darcy wasn't sure she had the focus or energy to deal with this, but as an attorney she knew it could be critical to the investigation.

"Do you think Marlene helped your father plan the kidnapping?" she asked, shifting Noah in her arms so she could face Adam head-on.

Adam didn't answer right away. He squeezed his eyes shut and groaned. "It's possible. It's also possible my father stole the money from the safe. He was there. I let him in myself, and I know he was in my mother's office."

"Did you see him take it?" Darcy pressed.

"No. But he had my mother's briefcase with him when he left the house." Adam opened his eyes and met her stare. "He could have used that seventy-five thousand to fund the kidnapping."

Grayson and Dade exchanged glances, and it was Grayson who stepped forward, right next to Darcy. "Why do you think that?" he asked Adam.

Again, Adam took several seconds to answer. "I heard him on the phone speaking to someone in Spanish. I don't speak the language myself, but I heard him say *pistolero*. I looked it up on the internet, and it means—"

"Gunman," Darcy and Grayson said in unison.

That admission changed everything. Father and son

were no longer in the camp of accusing Dent, and now Adam had just pinned both means and opportunity on his father. Edwin already had motive—revenge against his ex for divorcing him and marrying a much younger man. Plus, he had to be worried that Dent would cut off his allowance the moment he inherited Sandra's estate.

"I'll go upstairs with Grace and Kimmie," Mel volunteered. She took Noah from Darcy.

"I'll be up soon," Darcy let her know. But first she wanted to ask Adam a few more questions. "Why didn't you tell us this before now?"

"I didn't know about Marlene until today." He dodged her gaze. "And I didn't want to...believe my father could do something like this to my mother. Even though they were divorced, my parents were still in love, in their own way. It would have crushed my mother to know he was carrying on with a woman like Marlene."

Adam sounded sincere enough. There was even a slight quiver in his voice, especially when he said *my mother*. And maybe he did love her, even though after interviewing Sandra's so-called friends and family, Darcy was having a hard time believing that anyone actually loved the woman. But plenty of people loved her money. Of course, Adam would only benefit financially if his stepfather was convicted of the murder. Not his father.

But Darcy rethought that. Could Edwin benefit somehow?

It certainly wasn't an angle she'd researched, but she made a mental note to do just that. Maybe it was the kidnapping or Ramirez's escape, but she wasn't in a trusting mood.

"My father said Marlene is crazy in love with him," Adam went on. "Emphasis on the *crazy*. I think she'd do anything for him, with or without his consent. She might have believed this was a way to get him back in her life."

Darcy looked back at Grayson to see if he shared the same opinion, but the sheriff only lifted his shoulder. *Mercy.* That meant this investigation was about to head out on a new tangent. She didn't mind that in itself, but the more tangents, the longer it might take to figure out who was creating the danger and make an arrest.

"Put all of this in writing," Grayson told Adam. The sheriff pointed toward the paper and pen that were already on the table.

When Adam went back inside the interview room, Grayson shut the door. "Adam will have to wait. I've already asked for a check on Marlene's financials, but I doubt the woman had the money to hire gunmen."

True. After all, she worked at a day care and preschool. "Can you run Edwin's financials, too?" Darcy asked.

"Yeah." And Grayson didn't ask why, which meant he'd already considered that money might be playing into Adam's bombshell about his father's possible guilt. He tipped his head to the back stairs. "There's an apartment on the second floor where Mel and Grace took the children. Why don't you wait up there with them?"

Darcy wasn't about to argue with that, but before she could head in that direction, the back door flew open and someone walked in.

Nate.

She felt herself moving. Running toward him. Yes, it was stupid with his brother and heaven knows who else around. But she went to him. And was more than surprised when Nate closed the distance between them and pulled her into his arms.

"I'm okay," he whispered.

It was the same thing Grayson had told her, but this time she believed it. Still, the panic already had hold of her. Her breath broke, and Darcy disgraced herself by crying. Nate came to the rescue again and wiped the tears from her cheeks.

His hands were already damp. His hair, too. And the rain had soaked his shirt.

"How are the children?" Nate asked. He leaned down, cupped her face and looked her straight in the eyes.

It was the one subject that could get her to focus. "They're fine."

"Good." He pushed her hair from her face and brushed a kiss on her mouth. His lips were also wet from the rain. "Don't worry. We'll find Ramirez."

Again, she believed him and wished she could stay longer in his arms. But the sound of footsteps had them pulling apart. It was Grayson, and even though Darcy felt better, it was clear that Nate's brother didn't share her relief. No doubt because of the kiss he'd just witnessed.

"Where's Mason?" Grayson practically growled.

Nate kept his arm around her waist, causing Grayson's gaze to drop in that direction. "At the ranch, waiting for the rangers and the FBI," Nate told him. "After they arrive, he's driving Bessie to her sister's house."

Darcy hated that she was causing this tension between Nate and his brother, but she would hate even more having to distance herself from Nate. This attraction probably couldn't lead anywhere, but she wasn't ready to let go of it just yet.

Grayson continued to stare at the embrace for several moments. Then he mumbled something and headed back down the hall, saying what he had to say over his shoulder. "I have Adam Frasier in an interview room writing a statement. Darcy can fill you in on what's happening."

Well, at least Grayson hadn't said her name as if it were profanity.

"Adam says now that his father could be behind the kidnapping. Or Marlene," she explained. "Grayson is already digging to see if it's true. Or if Adam is just trying to cover up his own guilt."

Nate wearily shook his head. "Maybe when we catch Ramirez, we can get him to talk."

Darcy was about to remind him that at best Ramirez was a long shot, but then she heard the voices. One familiar voice in particular.

Wesley Dent.

She turned and spotted him making his way down the hall toward them. Tina, the dispatcher, was right behind him, telling him that he would have to wait in reception.

"It's okay, Tina," Nate assured the woman, and he stepped in front of Darcy. Probably because Dent looked riled enough to explode.

"You'd better not be here to threaten Darcy again," Nate warned.

"No threat. I'm here because I found something." Dent started to reach into his jacket pocket, and before he could get his hand inside, Nate had his gun drawn and pointed it right at the man.

Dent glanced at the gun. Then Nate. Dent looked as if he tried to smirk, but he failed. "I'm not the killer, Lieutenant Ryland." Now, he managed some smugness. "But I have something that could blow your investigation wide open."

That got her attention. Nate's, too. And Dent waited until Nate eased his gun back down before he reached into his pocket and extracted a small black leather-bound book. One look and Darcy immediately knew what it was.

Sandra Dent's missing diary.

"Read it," Dent said, thrusting it toward Nate. "And then you'll know who killed my wife."

Chapter Twelve

Nate didn't touch the diary, but he figured if this was the real deal, then any fiber or print evidence on it had already been compromised.

Still, they might get lucky.

With Grayson and Darcy right behind them, Nate led Dent into Grayson's office, took a sterile plastic evidence bag from the supply cabinet and placed it on the center of the desk. Nate motioned for Dent to place the diary there.

"Where did you find it?" Nate asked Dent. But he didn't look at the man. He grabbed a plastic glove, as well, and lifted the diary's cover.

"In the back of Sandra's closet. It'd been shoved into a coat pocket."

Nate was certain the cops had gone through Sandra's closet, but it was possible they'd missed it.

"Go to the last entry," Dent instructed.

Nate did, and Darcy and Grayson moved closer so they could look, as well. The handwritten words practically jumped off the page.

Adam and I argued tonight again. Money, always money. He's too much like his father. Let's see how sorry he is when his allowance is gone.

"Sandra was about to cut off Adam's allowance," Dent emphasized.

Nate mentally went back through his notes. Adam's allowance was a hundred thousand a year and was paid out through a trust fund, but it was a trust fund with strings. Adam could only get the hundred grand per year and that was it. He couldn't touch the principal amount itself for any reason.

A hundred thousand wasn't a huge sum by Sandra's standards, but maybe this was motive for Adam to kill her—especially since the allowance would have continued for the rest of his life. Well, it would continue unless Sandra managed to disown him and rewrite the conditions of the trust.

"Adam didn't say anything about this during his interview," Grayson mumbled, the disgust and frustration in his voice.

Nate understood that frustration. This case just kept getting more complicated, and they had to find the culprit soon so they could end the danger for the children.

"Adam's still here," Grayson added. "I need to talk to him again."

When Grayson walked out, Nate stayed and continued with the diary, but he quickly realized the page was the last thing Sandra had written. He checked the date at the top.

The night before she died.

Well, the timing was suspect. But then Nate noticed something else. The ragged edge, barely visible, indicating a subsequent page had been ripped out.

Nate looked up at Dent. "Know anything about this missing page?"

Dent seemed surprised by the question and had a look for himself. "No. I didn't see that until now. Maybe Adam tore it out?"

"You'd like them to think that, wouldn't you?" Adam snarled from the hall.

With Grayson right behind him, Adam marched into the room and looked at the diary. When he reached for it, Nate blocked his hand.

"It's evidence now," Nate informed him. "I'll have it couriered to the SAPD crime lab for immediate analysis." He pointed to the blank page beneath the one that had been torn out. "I think we might have impressions so we can figure out what your mother wrote."

Both Dent and Adam went deadly silent. For a few seconds, anyway.

"We don't even know if that is my mother's diary," Adam concluded.

"True," Nate acknowledged. "But we have her handwriting on file. It shouldn't take long for the lab to do a comparison."

The muscles in Adam's jaw turned to iron, and he snapped toward Dent. "You're setting me up." He whirled back to Nate. "Yes, my mother and I argued, but we worked out everything before someone murdered her."

"I didn't kill her," Dent calmly replied. He seemed to be enjoying Adam's fit of temper.

"Well, someone did. Either you or my father." Adam poked him in the chest with his index finger. "And if it was you, then I'm going to prove it."

That washed away Dent's calm facade, and Nate was concerned the two men might come to blows. He was too tired to break up a fight. "Are you done with Adam?" he asked Grayson.

His brother nodded.

"Both of you can leave," Nate told Dent and Adam.

"But what about the diary?" Adam demanded.

"We'll let you know what the lab says."

"And then they can arrest you," Dent concluded. He smiled and walked out.

Adam cursed him, but he didn't rush after his stepfather. "Don't let him get away with murder," Adam demanded.

Nate huffed and motioned for him to leave. For a moment, he thought Adam might argue, but the man finally stormed out.

Grayson put on a pair of gloves and picked up the diary. "I'll have Tina fax the pages to the crime lab so they can do a quick comparison of the handwriting to make sure it's Sandra Dent's. Then, I'll have a courier pick it up."

Nate thanked him, and once Grayson was out of the room, he turned his attention to Darcy. She looked several steps beyond exhaustion. And worried. Because he thought they could both use it, he brushed a kiss on her mouth.

Yeah, he needed it, all right, and wasn't surprised that the kiss worked its magic and soothed him.

Man, he was toast.

"Why don't you go check on the kids?" he suggested. "I need to make some calls."

She didn't question that. Darcy only nodded, turned but then turned back. She kissed him. Like his, it was brief, barely a touch, but she pulled back with her forehead bunched up and a frown on that otherwise tempting mouth.

"We'll deal with this later," he promised, figuring she knew exactly what he meant. The only question was how they would deal with it.

Except that wasn't in question, either.

They'd deal with it in bed. With some good old-fashioned sex. And yeah, it would mess things up with his family. It might even become the final straw of stress that would break his proverbial back. But Nate was certain that sex would happen no matter how it messed up things.

She ran her hand down the length of his arm. "Just yell if you want me," Darcy whispered.

Despite the fatigue, he smiled. So did she—after she blushed.

Nate watched her walk away. He felt the loss, or something. And wondered when the heck Darcy had become such an important part of his life. Cursing himself and cursing her, he pushed that question aside and got to work. He called Sergeant Garrett O'Malley at SAPD headquarters, the cop working on the Dent case. And now the kidnapping, as well.

"Garrett," Nate greeted. "What do you have on Marlene Lambert's financials?"

"There's nothing much in her checking account, but something else popped up," he explained, and in the background was the sound of the sergeant typing on a computer keyboard. "Two months ago she sold some land she'd inherited from her grandparents. The buyer gave her a check for nearly fifty thousand, which she cashed, but that fifty grand hasn't shown up in her financial accounts."

Nate felt the knot twist in his stomach. This was a woman he'd known for a long time. A woman he'd trusted with the safety and care of his baby girl.

"Of course, Ms. Lambert might have a good explanation," Garrett went on, "but I'm not seeing it right now."

So, Nate knew what had to be done. Grayson would have to bring her back in for questioning and grill her until she told them everything. Fifty thousand probably wasn't enough to have pulled off the entire kidnapping plot, but it would have been enough to get it started.

"What about the financials on Edwin and Adam Frasier?" Nate asked. "I wanted someone to take a harder look at those."

"I did," Garrett assured him. "And if either of them spent an unexplained chunk of money from any of their accounts, I can't find it."

Those financials had been a long shot since neither man would have been stupid enough to have the money trail lead straight back to them. Especially when Adam or Edwin could have just stolen that money from the safe. But Nate had still hoped he could pin this on one of them. On anyone. He just needed this to end.

"I did see something that might be important," Garrett said a moment later. "Adam is the sole heir to his father's estate, and while Edwin doesn't have a lot of cash, he does own a house that he got from the divorce settlement. It's worth close to two million. If something happened to Edwin—jail, death, whatever— Adam would be executor of his father's estate."

Interesting. Nate was betting Edwin would do something about that now that his son had implicated him in the kidnapping. It was also interesting that if either Dent or Edwin went down for Sandra's murder, then Adam would benefit.

Yeah. That was motive, all right.

Of course, Dent had just as big a motive. And Nate couldn't discount Edwin's jealousy of his ex-wife's new boy toy. Or Marlene's possible misguided love.

In other words, he was still at square one. All four of his suspects had motives, and worse, they could have had the means and opportunity, as well.

Nate thanked the sergeant, hung up and was about to check on Darcy and the children, but Grayson was right outside the door. Waiting. And judging from his brother's expression, something bad had happened.

"The children?" Nate automatically asked.

"Are fine," Grayson assured him. He stretched his hand across his forehead and ground his thumb and finger into his temples. "But I'm thinking we need to get them to a safe house."

That nearly knocked the breath out of Nate. "What happened?"

Grayson tipped his head in a follow-me gesture and started toward the front of the building to the dispatcher's desk, where Tina was packaging the diary for the courier.

"Did you find something in the diary?" Nate demanded.

"No. But Tina did fax copies, so we might know something soon." Grayson went toward the computer on Tina's desk. "While you were on the phone, I got a call from Kade. About twenty minutes ago, Ramirez was spotted on a security camera at a gas station off the highway. Less than five miles from town."

Oh, mercy. That was way too close for comfort. "Is Kade going out there to try to arrest him?"

Grayson shook his head. "Ramirez is already gone." He turned the computer monitor so Nate could see the feed from the security camera.

Yeah. It was Ramirez, all right, standing under the sliver of the overhanging roof of the gas station. And he wasn't alone. There was another broad-shouldered man with him. Both were wearing baseball caps and raincoats, but the bulkiness in their pockets indicated they were carrying weapons.

"We have this image and a description of the vehicle," Grayson pointed out, tapping the black four-door sedan stopped in front of the gas station.

But not just parked. It was directly in the line of sight of the security camera. Nate watched as Ramirez looked up at the camera.

Ramirez smiled.

The anger slammed through him, and Nate wished he could reach through the screen and teach this moron a hard lesson about endangering babies.

"What's he doing there, anyway?" Nate asked. Because it was clear Ramirez wasn't filling up the car or buying something.

"He's leaving a message," Grayson mumbled.

Yeah. That was obvious. "And that message is he's begging for me to go after him."

"Not quite."

Since Nate hadn't expected to hear Grayson say that, he snapped toward him. "What do you mean?"

"Just watch," Grayson instructed.

Nate did, and his heart started to ram against his chest. Within seconds, Ramirez pulled a folded piece of paper from his raincoat pocket, lifted it toward the camera and then tucked it into the glass door. He gave the camera one last smile, and the men got into the vehicle and sped away.

Not quietly.

The tires howled against the wet concrete and created enough noise to get the clerk's attention. The young man hurried to the door, opened it and caught the note before it dropped to the ground. He read it, his eyes widening with each passing second, and then he raced back into the station and grabbed the phone.

"The clerk called nine-one-one," Grayson supplied. "And in turn the dispatcher called here. He read me the note." Grayson took the notepad from the desk and handed it to Nate.

He knew this wouldn't be good, and Nate tried to brace himself for the worst.

But the message turned Nate's blood to ice.

Nate Ryland and Darcy Burkhart, you killed my brother and my men. This is no longer a job. It's personal, and I'm coming after both of you. Get ready to die.

"Uh, guys," Tina said, "I think we have a problem."

At first Nate thought she was talking about the note. Yeah, it was a problem, all right. A big one. But Tina was looking out the window.

"There." Tina tipped her head to the building just up the street.

The rain was spitting on the glass, but Nate could still see the shadowy figure using the emergency ladder on the side of the hardware store. The guy was climbing onto the roof.

And Nate reached for his gun.

"Wait," Grayson warned. "The windows here are tinted. He can't see us to shoot inside."

Grayson was right. Besides, the guy wasn't in a shooting stance. Once he reached the roof, he dropped onto his belly and pressed binoculars to his eyes.

"Recognize him?" Grayson asked.

Yeah. Nate did. It was the man who'd been with Ramirez on the surveillance footage. Nate automatically glanced around, looking for the man who'd just threatened to kill Darcy and him.

But Ramirez was nowhere in sight.

"You going out there?" Tina asked them.

"No," Grayson and Nate said in unison.

"Not right now," Nate finished.

Good. Grayson and he were on the same page, and Nate knew what he had to do. Darcy wasn't going to like it. Heck, *he* didn't like it. But it was necessary if he had any chance of keeping all of them out of the path of a killer.

Chapter Thirteen

Darcy read the note again. And again.

Each time it felt as if the words were razor-sharp knives slicing through her. A monster, a cold-blooded killer, was coming after Nate and her.

"I won't let him get to you," she heard Nate say.

Darcy believed that Nate would try. But Ramirez wasn't just after her. He was after Nate, as well.

She tore her attention from the note and looked at Nate, who was seated next to her. He'd made her sit on the sofa in the second-floor apartment at the sheriff's office before he'd handed her the note, and that was probably a good thing. After reading it, her legs were too wobbly to stand.

"We have a plan," Grayson explained. He was standing, his hands on his hips. Grace was behind him, seated on the floor and playing with the babies, trying to keep them occupied.

"Please tell me that plan includes making sure the children are safe." Darcy's voice cracked, and she hated feeling scared out of her mind for Noah and Kimmie. Nate, too.

"It does," Nate assured her. "We're going to set a

trap for Ramirez." He caught her shoulders and waited until they'd made eye contact. "And I'll be the bait."

Oh, mercy. That required her to take a deep breath. Thankfully, Grayson continued so she didn't have to ask about the details of this plan, which she already knew she didn't like. She wouldn't approve of anything where Nate made himself bait.

"First, we've made arrangements to move Grace, you and the children. We'll secretly take all of you to a safe house in a neighboring town, where both Mel and I will be with them. So will the town's sheriff and the deputy."

Okay. The security was a good start, but it wasn't enough. Maybe nothing would be with Nate's life at stake. And that required another deep breath.

"Secretly," Nate repeated. "Someone is watching the building."

"Who?" she immediately wanted to know. "Not Ramirez?" Darcy would have jumped off the sofa if Nate hadn't kept hold of her.

"No. It's a man who was on the surveillance video with him. Right now, he's on the roof of the hardware store just up the street. The dispatcher spotted him there about an hour ago. Once we knew he was there, Grayson and I sat down and came up with this plan."

Darcy shook her head. "Why don't you just arrest him? Make him tell you where Ramirez is."

"We considered it," Grayson explained. "But we figured the guy would die before giving up his boss. And we don't want a gunfight with the children here. So we decided to make it work for us."

"How?" she wanted to know.

"Soon, it'll be dark, and Nate will pretend to leave.

It's raining so we'll give him a big umbrella and bundles of something to carry. It'll look as if he has the children with him, but actually we'll sneak them and you out through the back and into my SUV. Kade will be here as additional protection just in case this guy comes off the roof. But we don't think he will."

Darcy tried to think that through. She wished her thoughts would settle down so she could figure out why this sounded so wrong. "You think he'll report to Ramirez that Nate's left and then he'll follow him?"

Nate nodded. "He'll follow me to the ranch. Ramirez will, too, and that's where we'll set the trap for them."

"The ranch?" she challenged. Now, she came off the sofa. "Your family is there."

Nate stood, slowly, and stuffed his hands into his pockets. "We've already moved them. Eve, Kayla and Kayla's son, Robbie, are already on their way to SAPD headquarters, where they'll stay until this situation with Ramirez is resolved."

Yes. And it wouldn't be resolved until Ramirez was dead. Darcy got that part, and she got other things, too. "There's a big flaw in your plan," she told them, even though they already knew it. "If Ramirez wants us both dead, then he won't be satisfied just trying to kill you. He'll want to come after me, as well."

Nate attempted a shrug but didn't quite pull it off. "He might."

"He *will,*" Darcy corrected. "And if Ramirez gets lucky and finds me, he'll find the children, too."

Neither Grayson nor Nate could deny that. "We won't let Ramirez get near them."

Darcy took a deep breath and braced herself for the argument they were about to have. An argument she would win because there was no way she was going to give Ramirez a reason to go after Kimmie and Noah again.

"There's only one thing that makes sense—for both of us to lead Ramirez away from the children. Anything less than that puts them in danger."

Nate's jaw muscles stirred. "But coming with me puts you in danger."

"Yes." And she didn't hesitate. "We know what has to be done here. You don't have to like it. Heck, I don't like it. But I won't be tucked away at a safe house knowing that I could be putting our children in jeopardy."

He opened his mouth, probably to continue the argument, but Darcy nipped it in the bud. "You can't change my mind. I'm going with you."

Nate looked at Grayson, who only huffed and mumbled something. Nate looked as if he wanted to mumble some profanity, but he didn't. He sat down, his jaw muscles battling, and then he finally nodded.

Darcy tried not to look too relieved. It was easy to do, since she knew full well she was putting herself in the line of fire. Still, better her than the babies.

Nate simply nodded again. "If Ramirez knows we're at the ranch, he'll come after us so he can try to avenge his kid brother's death. But we'll be ready for him."

"How?" she asked.

Nate eased her down onto the sofa, but they both glanced back when the children giggled. Grace was reading them a story and making funny voices. The laughter certainly helped Darcy's nerves and reminded her of why this plan had to work.

"We think the man on the roof is the person who

helped Ramirez escape. We also believe he's the one who called Ramirez when he climbed over the fence. He probably told his boss to get out of there because he'd seen Dade and Mel driving out of the ranch. In other words, he's Ramirez's eyes and ears, and we want to feed this guy some info."

"Bad info," Grayson explained. "We want Ramirez to believe this storm has knocked out both the power and the security system for the ranch. We want him to come across that fence again. And when he does, we'll have Kade and a half-dozen federal agents waiting."

Darcy nodded but then thought of something. "What if Ramirez doesn't use the fence? What if he uses the road and comes directly to the house?"

"Mason and I will be waiting for him," Nate assured her. "And if he's managed to hire more goons to come with him, then we'll know because Kade will have someone watching the road." He paused again. "It's the fastest way to put an end to this."

She couldn't argue with that. Darcy couldn't argue with the plan, either. Nate was a good cop, and she trusted him with her life. But she couldn't discount that Ramirez was as driven to kill them as they were to stay alive and keep their children safe.

"How much time before you and the children leave for the safe house?" she asked Grayson.

He glanced out the window. "Not long."

So, she needed to say her goodbyes. Darcy got up, forcing her legs to move, and she got down on the floor next to the children. Both Noah and Kimmie were still involved with the story, but Noah climbed into her lap. Kimmie babbled some happy sounds and did the same.

Everything was suddenly better.

And worse.

They had so much at stake. Darcy hugged the babies close to her. Kimmie might have sensed something was wrong because she kissed Darcy on the cheek and put her head on Darcy's shoulder. The moment was pure magic, and Darcy realized she'd come to love this child as her own.

"I'll just freshen up and get ready for the drive to the safe house," Grace offered, and she disappeared into the bathroom, no doubt to give them some time alone.

Grayson mumbled something about having to make some calls and walked out, as well.

Nate sat down beside her, and Darcy expected Kimmie to switch to his lap, but she stayed put. It was Noah who made the shift when he spotted Nate's shoulder holster. But Nate distracted her son by unclipping his badge from his belt and handing it to Noah.

"Oooo," Noah babbled, obviously approving of the shiny object. He looked up at Nate and offered him a big grin.

The moment hit Darcy hard, partly because her son had never had a male figure in his life, and partly because everything seemed to fit. Kimmie in her arms. Noah in Nate's. Her heart and body, burning for this man.

A man she couldn't have.

Nate was just now healing from his wife's death, and he needed his family to help him and Kimmie through the rest of that process. She couldn't put that wedge between them.

She kissed the top of Kimmie's head and ran her fingers through those fiery curls. The little girl had her mother's looks, but that smile and those silver-gray eyes were genetic contributions from her daddy.

"Me," her son said, and he handed the badge to Kimmie. "Me," he repeated.

"I think he's trying to say her name." Nate smiled.

But the smile and the moment ended when Nate's cell phone buzzed. He took the phone from his pocket and glanced at the screen.

"It's the SAPD crime lab." Nate put the call on speaker. "Lieutenant Ryland," he answered.

"Sir, we got that handwriting comparison you requested on the faxed pages," the tech said. "It's a match to the sample of handwriting we have for the deceased, Sandra Dent."

So, the diary was real. Of course, that created more questions than answers. Had Dent really just found it, or had he known all along where it was?

"The handwriting is consistent through all the pages," the tech added.

And that meant Sandra had written the entry about quarreling with her son and planning to cut him out of her life. Maybe Adam knew that. Maybe not. But Dent might have just given them a motive for Adam to kill his mother.

"What about the pages that were torn out?" Nate asked.

"We can't get anything from the paper itself. There's not even any partial letter there, but there could be some DNA or trace fibers. The lab has it now and has started the testing. They're also looking at the indentations on the pages following the ones that'd been torn out."

"And?" Nate prompted.

"It doesn't look good, Lieutenant. It appears someone has actually rubbed or applied pressure to flatten out the indentations, but the lab will do what it can."

Nate wearily dragged his hand over his face, but then smiled when Noah attempted to do the same. "Call me if you find out anything else," Nate instructed the tech, and he ended the call.

The phone grabbed Kimmie's attention, and she dropped Nate's badge so she could go after it. Just like that, Nate had both kids in his lap, and he adjusted, giving them both room, as if it were second nature for him. However, even the half smile he gave the children didn't mask his frustration.

"It would have been nice to know what Sandra wrote on that last page," Darcy said. "She might have named her killer, or at least given us some hint of who that person might be. I mean, why else would the pages have been torn out?"

Nate didn't answer her, but something flashed through his eyes. He took out his phone again and put it on speaker.

"Grayson," he said when his brother answered. "Is our guest still on the roof of the hardware store?"

"Still there. He's getting soaked, but he hasn't moved."

Darcy hoped he'd stay put. And catch pneumonia.

"I just finished talking with the lab," Nate explained to his brother. "The handwriting matches Sandra's, but the indentations probably won't give us anything. What I want is for all four of our suspects to believe otherwise. I want them to think the lab uncovered what Sandra had written and that SAPD is making arrangements for an arrest."

Grayson made a sound to indicate he was contemplating the idea. Darcy thought about it, too. If it worked, they could have Sandra Dent's killer in custody within hours.

"You think this'll flush out her killer and cause him or her to go on the run?" Grayson asked Nate.

"Yeah, I do. But I don't think it'll cause the killer to come after Darcy, me or the children again. He or she must have figured out by now that they can't use us to fix the murder investigation."

Grayson made a sound of agreement. "I'll make some calls and have the roads and airports watched. And then we'll have to make the suspects believe that one of them is about to be outed. That'll be easy to do for Marlene since she's already here."

"Why?" Darcy and Nate asked in unison.

"Your guess is as good as mine, but she's insisting that she talk to Darcy and you, too."

Nate groaned and looked at her. "You up for this?"

Darcy nodded. She didn't want to waste any more time with Marlene, but the woman might actually be there to confess to orchestrating the kidnapping. If she was, then Darcy very much wanted to hear what she had to say.

Darcy gave both babies a kiss, and Nate did the same. Then she knocked on the bathroom door to signal Grace should come out. Once Grace was back on the floor with the kids, Nate and Darcy headed downstairs to confront Marlene.

They didn't have to go far.

Marlene was in the hall, just outside of Grayson's office, and the moment she spotted them, she walked toward them. Grayson stepped out of his office and joined them, too.

"I didn't help anyone kidnap your children," Marlene volunteered. "When I heard the kidnappers say they were taking us to the Lost Appaloosa, I wrote the initials so you'd find us."

"But the van where you wrote them was a decoy," Nate pointed out.

"I didn't know that, either. That's the van they put us in when they first took us, and then they moved us to another one. I wouldn't have done anything to help them take Noah and Kimmie, and you have to believe me."

"Maybe I will believe you," Nate told her, "if you'll explain what you did with the fifty thousand you got for selling the land you inherited."

Marlene flinched as if he'd slapped her. "That has nothing to do with the kidnapping."

Darcy folded her arms over her chest and stared at Marlene. "Then where's the money?"

Marlene looked around as if she wanted to be anywhere but there, and for a moment Darcy thought she might bolt. Would that mean Marlene was guilty?

"You're wasting our time," Nate accused.

Marlene shook her head, but it still took her several moments to say anything. "Someone's trying to kill me."

And she didn't add more. Just that little bombshell.

"Who's trying to kill you?" Darcy asked. "Ramirez?"

"No." But then Marlene paused. "Well, maybe it's him, but I don't think so. If he'd wanted me dead he could have killed me when I was his hostage."

"Were you?" Nate demanded, and then he clarified, "His hostage?"

"Yes. Those gunmen took me when they took the children, and it doesn't have anything to do with the money I got from selling the land."

Nate huffed. So did Grayson. "Look," Grayson warned, "either you explain about the money now, or I arrest you for obstruction of justice."

Marlene's eyes widened, and it seemed to hit her that she was in big trouble. "I gave the money to my sister in San Antonio." She paused again. "She was in debt to a man who was threatening to kill her. I had to pay him off."

Nate rolled his eyes. "Let me get this straight—someone's trying to kill both you and your sister, and not once did you consider telling Grayson about this?"

"I couldn't." Again, she shouted, but then she blinked back tears. "The loan shark would have killed my sister if she'd gone to the cops. And as for me, I don't think this man has anything to do with the threats on my life."

Darcy could practically feel the frustration coming off Grayson and Nate. She felt it, too, and only wanted this woman to spill it and get out of there. Soon, very soon, the children would be leaving for the safe house, and she wanted to spend a little more time with them.

"Explain why you think someone's trying to kill you," Grayson insisted, and it wasn't a gentle request.

Marlene hiked up her chin and clearly wasn't pleased that Grayson and Nate seemed to doubt her. If she was innocent, Darcy would apologize to the woman, but for now she wanted the same thing Nate and Grayson did—the truth.

"Someone's been following me," Marlene started. "And before the kidnapping, I was getting hang-ups."

Grayson, Nate and Darcy all looked toward the front of the building when the bell jangled, indicating someone had opened the front door. Nate stepped in front of Darcy. Grayson, too. And they both slid their hands over their guns.

Darcy held her breath, praying the man from the roof hadn't decided to come in and try to kill them. But the person who walked through the door was a familiar face, although not a welcome one.

It was Edwin.

He used his hand to swipe the rain from his face, and he stormed toward them. He didn't make it far. Tina, the dispatcher, stepped in front of him to block his path. Edwin did stop, but he aimed his index finger and a scowl at Marlene.

"Whatever she says, it's a lie," Edwin growled.

Marlene frantically shook her head. "It's true. Someone is trying to kill me. Or scare me at least. And I think it's *you*."

"Please." Edwin stretched out the syllables. "You were a cheap fling, nothing more, and I never gave you a minute's thought until that damn kidnapping."

Edwin's anger seemed genuine enough, and it seemed genuinely directed at Marlene. However, Darcy wasn't about to cross either of them off her list of suspects. Judging from Nate's expression, neither was he.

"Are you trying to kill her?" Nate asked him.

Edwin cursed. "She's not worth killing." He pointed at Marlene again. "I plan to do everything in my power to find proof that you set up the kidnapping so that Dent would be tossed in jail. Trust me, I want him in jail, but

I don't need or want your help for that. You're a stalking, obsessive wacko, and I want you out of my life."

Marlene opened her mouth, no doubt to return verbal fire, but Nate put up his hand in a *stop* motion. "In a few hours we'll know who killed Sandra."

Edwin and Marlene both seemed to freeze, and each stared at Nate. "What do you mean?" Marlene asked Nate.

"Dent found Sandra's diary—"

"It's a fake," Edwin interrupted.

Nate shook his head. "It's not. The lab just confirmed that the handwriting is hers."

His voice was so calm. He was all cop now, and Darcy watched as he took one menacing step closer to Marlene. But the woman wasn't the only one to earn some of his attention. Nate turned those suddenly cold gray eyes on Edwin, too.

"The next step is for the lab to lift the indentations Sandra made when she wrote the page that was torn out," Nate continued. "The page that sealed her fate and named her killer."

"Someone could have planted information to make me look guilty," Edwin snarled.

"Or me," Marlene piped up.

Nate lifted his shoulder again. "Then maybe you two should call your attorneys. Because I'm betting one or both of you will need a good lawyer before the night is over."

Edwin stood there, glaring, as if he would launch himself at Nate or Marlene, but then he cursed again, turned and walked back out into the rain.

"Excuse me," Grayson mumbled when his desk phone rang.

Marlene, however, didn't storm out with Edwin. In fact, she didn't budge an inch. "I believe Edwin is trying to scare me. Or worse." She groaned. "He's trying to make me look guilty because he's the one who put all of this together. He killed his ex-wife, and he wants Wesley Dent to go to jail because he hates him that much."

All of that could be true.

Or none of it.

"You got proof?" Nate asked.

Marlene groaned again, more softly this time, and she stared at Nate. "You really believe Sandra wrote her killer's name in her diary?"

"I do," Nate said, sounding totally confident.

"Good," Marlene whispered. Then she mumbled a goodbye and hurried down the hall.

Darcy didn't release the breath she'd been holding until Marlene was out the door.

"Lock it," Nate instructed Tina. "We've had enough surprise visitors today. Besides, I don't want anyone walking in when we're transferring the children into the van that will take them to the safe house."

Darcy shook her head. She'd thought it was too early for the children to leave, but she was wrong. It was still an hour or so before actual nightfall, but the rain and the iron-gray clouds made it seem like night.

The darkness was closing in.

And so was her fear.

Nate must have sensed what she was feeling because he gave her arm a gentle squeeze. He was still doing that when Grayson threw open his office door.

"Everything is ready for the children," Grayson told

them. There was both sympathy and concern in his voice. "It's time."

"Come on," Nate whispered to her. "We need to tell Kimmie and Noah goodbye."

Darcy swallowed hard. *Goodbye*. It hit her then that while their children would be safe, Nate wouldn't be. They would have to face the devil himself and somehow come out of it alive.

Or this was the last time they would ever see their children.

Chapter Fourteen

The plan was in place. Nate knew he'd done everything possible to make this work.

Well, *logically* he knew that.

But in the back of his mind, he hated that he couldn't guarantee all of them would come out of this unscathed.

He ended the call with Kade. One of many calls Nate had made over the past hour since Darcy and he had arrived at the ranch. More would no doubt have to be made.

"Well?" Darcy asked the moment he hung up.

She was in the doorway of his office, her hands bracketed on the door frame. All the lights in the house were off—that was part of their plan, to lure Ramirez with a fake power outage—but Nate didn't need to see her face to know she was worried and on edge. He could hear it in her voice. In that one word. In the air zinging around them. The storm brewing outside only added to the menacing feel.

"The children are fine," he assured her. "They're all tucked in for the night at the safe house."

Her breathing was way too fast, and he thought he could even hear her heartbeat. "Thank God," she whispered.

Nate echoed that. "So far none of our suspects has shown up at the airport or the border. None has withdrawn any money from their bank accounts. No suspicious activity of any kind even though Adam is out driving around. Dade is watching him, and we have surveillance on the others' houses."

Darcy shook her head. "But they could sneak out."

"They could," he admitted. "But if that happens, and the killer heads in this direction, we'll know. Kade and his men are scattering out all over the ranch to set up surveillance equipment."

"What about the man who was on the roof of the hardware store?" she asked.

"He left right after we did. On foot. He disappeared into the alley behind the stores."

That didn't help her breathing.

"We figure he's already joined up with his boss, Ramirez." He walked closer to her. "When all the equipment is set up and everything is in place, the ranch hands will pretend there's an emergency. A fence down from the storm. And they'll appear to leave the area. If Ramirez is watching the ranch, and we're almost positive he is, then he'll believe that's his opportunity to strike."

Her breath shivered, and Nate pulled her into his arms. It wasn't much of a hug, but it helped to relax her. Him, too. But it didn't help the attraction.

Not a good time for it.

But then, there'd never been a good time.

"Why don't you try to get some rest?" he said softly. Trying to stay calm. Trying not to let her hear the concern in his own voice.

A burst of air left her mouth. Not exactly a laugh.

"Rest? Right." And then she did something that shouldn't have surprised him. But it did.

Darcy put her arms around him and kissed him. Not a peck of reassurance. Not this. The kiss was long, hard and filled with way too much need. And urgency.

"Rest," he repeated. Not easily. That kiss had made him crazy in a bad way. He was starting to think that kissing and maybe adrenaline sex might be the way to get through the waiting.

Darcy pulled back and hesitated. The moments crawled by while he waited for her response.

"Rest with me," she insisted.

An *okay* nearly flew right out of his mouth before he remembered he had to set up the surveillance on his laptop. Not that he would actually be able to see anything in the dark and rain, but the motion detectors were on, and he would get the alert over the laptop if Ramirez did come across any part of the fence. His brothers and the ranch hands already had equipment to detect movement, but Nate wanted it as a backup for himself. And in case something went wrong with the exterior detection equipment.

"I'll be in my room," Darcy added, and she walked away.

Nate stared at the empty doorway for a second. And he cursed himself for what he knew would happen before the night was over. He should have one thing on his mind: Ramirez. But Ramirez wouldn't get anywhere near the place without Nate and the others knowing.

There was time to kill.

Or so he rationalized.

He could kill that time in his office, waiting and

watching. He could stay away from Darcy and give her the possibility of getting some rest.

But that didn't happen.

Nate turned on his laptop and tapped into the security feed. It didn't take long for the images to appear on the screen. And just as he'd figured, nothing was going on. He couldn't see a thing in the rainy darkness so he tucked the laptop under his arm, took a deep breath and launched into what would no doubt be a very pleasurable but stupid mistake.

He walked straight to Darcy's room.

The door was open, and he stepped inside so he could put his laptop on the table just a few feet away. He took off his shoulder holster, as well, and dropped it next to the laptop.

Bright white lightning flashed through the rain-streaked window. For a second Nate saw Darcy sitting on the edge of the bed. Her ivory-colored top, her blond hair, her pale skin all made her look a little otherworldly. A siren, maybe. Or a rain goddess.

But then the darkness took over the room again.

He stood there, letting his eyes adjust, waiting for another jolt of lightning. He didn't have to wait long. It came. Stabbing across the sky and giving him another look at her. He felt starved for the sight of her.

And he groaned at that somewhat sappy realization.

"That bad, huh?" she asked.

He waited for the lightning again to see if she was smiling. She was. Well, sort of. "I'm thinking thoughts I don't usually think," he confessed. "Sappy ones."

He heard the mattress creak softly as she stood. Then heard her footsteps on the bare wood floor. "Good," she whispered.

Oh, man. Did she know how hot she sounded all breathy like that? Apparently, he was starved for the sound of her voice, too.

"Good?" he challenged when he remembered how to form words with his mouth. His body didn't want to contribute any energy to something that didn't involve getting Darcy naked. "You want me to think sap?"

She stepped closer so he could see the half smile, and her face. "You've done a number on my mind. My body. I figure it's only fair that you're sappily confused."

Nate sighed and slipped his arm around her waist. "Oh, I'm not confused, Darcy. I know exactly what I want—and that's *you.*"

The slam of thunder gave his confession a little more punch than he'd intended, and Darcy laughed. It was smoky and rich, and Nate kissed her so he could feel that laughter on his lips.

"Good," she repeated. "Because I want *you.*"

Yeah. He knew that.

And that was the problem. Neither was going to stop this getting-naked part. Ditto for some raunchy, memorable sex. The door was locked. They had some privacy for the first time in, well, forever. And even though there would be hell to pay, Nate eased her to him and deepened the kiss.

Later, he would pay hell.

Now, he just wanted to kiss her blind. For starters, anyway.

There was something about her, about that taste, that made him crazier than he already was, and he felt his body rev up to take her hard and fast.

Especially hard.

He considered something mindless, maybe even

sex against the wall. Sex where he didn't have to think of the consequences. But a rain goddess who tasted like sin deserved something better than that. And Nate wasn't surprised that he wanted to make love to her.

He leaned back, to make sure there wasn't any doubt in her eyes or expression. He could see her face, the rain shadows sliding down her body. She was beautiful. But he hadn't needed to see her face to remember that.

Nate scooped her up and headed for the bed. Even in this position, she fit, as if she belonged there in his arms. In his bed. Heck, maybe his life. He pushed that aside. It was too deep and too complicated to deal with now.

The lightning came again. And the thunder. As he eased her onto the bed, the mattress creaked softly and creaked some more when he followed on top of her. This fit, as well, and so did the way their mouths came together for the kiss.

It didn't take long, barely seconds, for the kisses to give way to touches. Darcy started it by sliding her hand down his chest. That did it all right. The simple, easy pressure of her hands on his body. And just like that, he was hard and aching to take her.

"You're like a fantasy," she whispered.

Despite his rock-hard body, Nate lifted his head to see what she meant by that.

"You are," she insisted. She didn't stop touching him or kissing his neck, and because she was apparently going for torture, she lifted her hips, brushed against the front of his jeans and caused his eyes to cross. "As in you're really hot. The kind of guy I always fantasized about…well, you know, in bed."

He couldn't imagine that he looked hot with crossed

eyes and the hard ache behind the zipper of his jeans, but at the moment he was just pleased that she wanted him as much as he wanted her. Especially since she was fulfilling a few of his own fantasies.

Her top had to go—more of his fantasy fulfillment—and Nate stripped it off. Her bra, too. And he kissed her breasts the way he wanted to kiss her, his tongue circling her nipple.

That brought her hips off the bed again, and she made a sweet sound of pleasure. A sound that slid right over him like the warm rain on the cool glass.

"You, too," Darcy insisted. And she went after his shirt.

While she fumbled with the buttons, Nate did some more sampling. He moved his mouth to her stomach and smiled when she made more of those pleasure sounds.

"I'm on fire," she let him know and gave his shirt a fierce tug.

Nate was pleased about that fire he'd helped build. Until her lips went to his chest. Oh, man. She wasn't a rain goddess. She was a witch, casting a spell with that mouth and setting him on fire.

When he could take no more of the scalding pleasure, he dropped to his side, pulling her on top of him so he could rid her of her jeans. Darcy didn't help much, mainly because she went after his zipper. He was hard and very aware of her touch.

Again, when he could take no more, he put her back on the mattress and shimmied her jeans and panties off.

The lightning cooperated.

Oh, yeah. She was beautiful all right, and Nate kissed her right in the center of all that heat.

She made another sound. This one had an urgency to it, but she didn't stop him. Darcy wound her fingers deep into his hair and took everything he was giving her.

Nate considered finishing her off like this, but he wanted more. He wanted to be inside her so he could watch and feel her shatter all around him.

"Your jeans," Darcy reminded him.

He was painfully aware that his remaining clothes were in the way of sex, and Nate helped her get off his boots and jeans.

But Darcy didn't play fair.

She was the one who removed his boxers, and she did it by sliding her hands down his lower back and his butt. And she didn't just use her hands. She used her knees and legs, and when she was done, when his boxers were dangling on her foot, she wrapped her legs around him.

Nate moved down as she moved up, and he slid into that tight, wet heat of her body. Stars. Yeah, he saw them. Hell, maybe fireworks, too. There was something exploding in his head, and the pleasure, well, it was something he was glad he didn't have to put into words.

He moved deep and hard inside her. But he didn't stop kissing her. Couldn't. After being so long without, he wanted it all. The taste of her in his mouth. Her scent on his skin. The feel of the hot, intimate contact of their sex.

"A fantasy," she repeated. Her eyes were wide, and she was staring at him.

Yes, it felt good enough to be her fantasy, and in the back of his mind he wondered if anything would ever feel this good again. But then the need took over, and his mind cleared of any thoughts except one.

Finishing this.

Turned out that was Darcy's goal, as well, because she met his thrusts, using her legs to pull him right back in. Over and over. Robbing him of his breath. Maybe his mind. Everything. Until all he could see and feel was Darcy.

She dug her fingers into his back when she climaxed, bucked beneath him, and her breath was mixed with hoarse sobs of pleasure.

Nate listened and watched her as long as he could. Cataloging every sound. Every move. Every expression. Until he could take no more. Until the ripples of her climax forced him into letting go.

The lightning came again. The thunder. And even over the thick rumble, Nate heard the single word he whispered.

"Darcy."

Chapter Fifteen

Darcy didn't want to move. Nor did she want to break the intimate contact with Nate.

But Nate apparently did.

He rolled off her and landed in a flop on his back. He didn't say anything, but Darcy could still hear the way he'd spoken her name in the last climactic moment.

Somehow, that had sounded more intimate than the sex itself.

In the back of her mind, she'd considered that Nate had been thinking about his late wife. That would have been, well, natural even though it was painful for her to consider. But it'd been Darcy's name on his lips. And he'd certainly made love to her as if she was the woman he wanted.

But did he?

Had this been a primal reaction to the danger?

She couldn't dismiss it, but she so wanted it to be real. She wanted Nate and not just his body—though Darcy wanted that, too.

And speaking of his body, she looked over at him. He was still naked, of course, and thanks to a jagged flash of lightning, she got a good look at him.

Oh, mercy.

Yes, she wanted to feel more of those toned muscles on his chest and stomach. More of his clever mouth and the kisses that could make her burn to ash. She wanted to be wrapped in his strong arms again. She wanted it all.

Darcy groaned and hoped the rumbling thunder concealed the sound that had escaped.

It didn't.

Nate tilted his head and looked at her. "Well?" he asked.

Sheesh. Where should she go with a question like that? Anything she said could make him regret what had just happened and might send him running for cover.

"Well," she repeated, giving herself some time to think, "the sex was amazing."

He stared at her. "Then why did you groan?"

That required another pause—and a deep breath. "Because this might have been easier for both of us if it hadn't been amazing."

Nate stayed quiet a moment and then made a sound of agreement. He brushed a kiss on her cheek, got up and started to dress.

Darcy wanted to smack herself for that stupid groan. It had reminded Nate of the trouble a possible relationship could stir up. That groan had broken the spell and caused him to move away from her.

Nate's phone buzzed, and he rifled through his clothes on the floor to find it. He glanced at the caller ID before he answered it.

"Kade," Nate answered.

Darcy prayed this was good news, but since Nate didn't put the call on speaker, she couldn't tell.

She got up, as well, and began to gather her clothes. Suddenly, Darcy felt awkward and uncomfortable about being stark naked in front of Nate. She dressed as quickly as she could. Not easy to do since her clothes were scattered everywhere.

"Did he have a suitcase or anything with him?" Nate asked his brother.

Again, she couldn't hear Kade's answer.

"A lot of people are watching the place," Nate responded. "If he shows up, we'll see him." And he hung up.

Darcy waited, her breath stalled in her lungs.

"It's Dent," Nate told her. "He left his house about a half hour ago, and he had a suitcase with him. He managed to lose the tail we had on him."

Darcy leaned against the wall and let it support her. She also put her hand over her breasts since she was still braless. Where was the darn thing?

"This doesn't mean Dent is a killer," Nate pointed out. He looked at her but then just as quickly turned away. "He could just be running scared."

True. But Darcy wasn't ready to trust Dent or any of the other suspects.

Nate finished dressing before her and went straight for his laptop, which he'd left on the table near the door. When he lifted the screen, it created a nightlight of sorts, and she was able to find her bra. It was dangling on the bedpost.

"No sign of Ramirez," he relayed to her, and he slipped his shoulder holster back on.

Ramirez. Just the thought of him chilled the remaining heat she felt after making love with Nate. How could she have forgotten, even for a few minutes, that a killer wanted them dead?

Sex with Nate wasn't just amazing.

It apparently caused temporary amnesia.

And stupidity.

Darcy finished dressing and saw that Nate was still staring at his laptop screen. "Is there a problem?" she said, praying there wasn't.

"No. I'm just reading an email from Grayson."

"Grayson?" She hurried across the room to see what the message said. "It's about the children?"

Of course, she immediately thought the worst, but what she saw on the screen wasn't the worst at all. There was a picture of both Kimmie and Noah. They were asleep side by side in a crib.

"Grayson snapped it with his cell phone and emailed it," Nate explained. "He thought it would make us feel better."

It did.

Darcy couldn't help herself. She touched the screen, running her fingers over those precious little faces. "I miss them so much."

"Them," Nate mumbled.

It hit her then that he might think she was trying to push her way into his life by using his daughter. Darcy frantically shook her head. "What I feel for Kimmie doesn't have anything to do with you."

He lifted his eyebrow and paused for what seemed an eternity, then nodded. "I know. You love kids." Nate added a shrug. "I love kids."

Darcy waited, but he offered nothing else. Especially nothing else about what he might be feeling for her. Or feelings about what had happened in that bed just minutes earlier. But because she was watching him so closely, she saw his expression change from that of a loving father to that of a very sad widower. He, too, touched the image on the screen, and Darcy suspected he was wishing that Ellie were alive.

"You miss your wife," Darcy said before she could stop herself.

"Yeah." No hesitation. Nate kept his gaze fixed on the screen for several seconds before he pulled back his hand and switched to the feed from the security system. He split the screen so that it showed six different camera angles at once.

She considered pushing a little and asking Nate to talk about his feelings. He'd no doubt rather eat razor blades than do that, so Darcy decided to give him the time and space to work out whatever was going on in his head. Heck, she needed that space, too.

But one look at the screen, and she realized her attention was going to be otherwise occupied. She saw movement in the top-left screen.

"Ramirez?" she managed to ask.

Unlike before, Nate didn't give her an immediate answer, but he did draw his gun from his shoulder holster. "I don't think so."

Whoever it was, the person wasn't on foot. Nor was he coming across the fence. This was a car, and the headlights were on, slicing through the thick rain. The vehicle was traveling on the ranch road.

Toward the house.

Oh, mercy. Darcy had thought she was ready for this. Well, as ready as anyone could be. But just the sight of that car made her heart spin out of control.

"I doubt Ramirez would drive right up to the front door," Nate added.

And that's exactly what the driver appeared to be doing. Darcy clung to that hope, that it wasn't Ramirez, but then she had to wonder, if it wasn't the killer, who was it? It was hardly the hour for guests, and all of Nate's brothers were occupied with either the children or setting the trap for Ramirez.

Nate's phone buzzed, and he answered it without taking his focus off the car. He clicked the speaker function.

"Nate," she heard Dade say. "Adam should be arriving at the ranch any minute now. I was tailing him, but I got…distracted. I spotted someone in the woods on the back side of the ranch, and I stopped. I think it might be our watcher from the roof. Can you deal with Adam on your own?"

"Sure," Nate answered. "What does Adam want?"

"Who knows. He checked into a hotel in Silver Creek, but about forty-five minutes ago, he came barreling out of the driveway like a man on fire. I guess he must have gone out to the parking lot through the emergency exit at the back of the hotel."

"Is he armed?" Nate wanted to know.

"Couldn't tell. I barely got a glimpse of him before he sped away from the hotel. I stayed back so he wouldn't spot me, but he didn't make it easy. He stopped on the side of the road twice, changed directions a couple of times, but then he finally headed out to the ranch."

"Any sign of Edwin, Dent or Marlene?" Nate asked.

"No. And I've been keeping my eye out for all of them in case they head out this way." In the background, Darcy could hear the storm winds howling. "You're positive you can handle Adam?"

"Don't worry about us. Just watch your back." Nate ended the call, picked up the laptop and started out of the room.

Darcy caught his arm. "You're not planning to let Adam in?"

"No. But I do want to talk to him. And I want to be closer to the door in case he decides to break in."

Darcy's grip melted off his arm. "Break in?" But she knew what Nate meant. Adam could have killed his mother, and the lie they'd planted about the diary could have sent him spinning out of control. With everything going on with Ramirez, she'd forgotten that someone had originally hired that monster to kidnap the children.

Was it Adam who'd done that?

And was he there to finish what he'd paid Ramirez to start?

Darcy followed Nate down the hall and toward the foyer, but he didn't go into the open area. Instead, he placed the laptop on the floor, and they crouched down where they could both still see it.

On the screen Darcy saw the car and then heard it come to a screeching halt. Adam certainly wasn't trying to conceal his arrival. Nate and she waited, watching, but Adam didn't get out. However, Nate's phone buzzed again, and when he flipped it open, it was Adam's name on the screen.

"What are you doing here?" Nate demanded when he answered the call. Darcy whispered for him to put it on speaker, and he did.

"I'm trying to stay alive, and you have to let me in. I

need to be in protective custody." Adam sounded scared out of his mind. Of course, Darcy knew it could all be an act.

"And you thought the way to stay alive was to come here?" Nate tossed right back.

Adam mumbled something she didn't catch. "Dent is trying to kill me. He murdered my mother, and now he's trying to kill me so he can inherit her entire estate and my trust fund. I want him arrested *now*."

"There's still no proof to arrest him. Or you, for that matter," Nate added. "But we might soon have proof with the diary."

"Yes," Adam mumbled. "The diary." He said it in the same tone as he would profanity. "Dent doctored that diary, and I'm betting he did that to make either me or my father look guilty of murder. When your lab people check those so-called indentations, they'll be fake, added by the real killer. And that real killer is Dent."

Darcy certainly couldn't discard that theory. But Dent had been the one to find the diary, and if her former client thought for one minute that it could have implicated him in his wife's murder, then he wouldn't have brought it to Grayson and Nate.

So, Dent was either innocent or stupid.

"If you really believe someone is trying to kill you," Nate said to Adam, "then go the sheriff's office or SAPD headquarters. Dent won't come after you there."

"No. But his hired gun would, and I'd rather have you protecting me than the deputy at the sheriff's office." Adam cursed. "I know Dent hired that psycho, Ramirez. He took the money from my mother's safe to pay him. And now he's hired Ramirez to come after me. And Darcy and you, too."

Nate glanced at her, and Darcy saw some doubt, but Nate wasn't totally dismissing what Adam had accused Dent of doing.

"What makes you think Ramirez is after you?" Nate demanded.

"I *know* he's after me. He came to my hotel room." Adam's voice cracked on the last word. "I'm sorry. He gave me no choice."

Darcy felt the icy chill go through her. "What do you mean?"

Adam took his time answering. "I mean Ramirez came here in the trunk of my car, and he got out just a few minutes ago—before we got to the security camera at the end of the road.

"I'm sorry," Adam repeated. "But Ramirez is on the grounds."

Chapter Sixteen

Nate prayed that Adam was lying. Or playing some kind of sick joke.

Yes, Nate was fully aware that Ramirez was after Darcy and him, but if Adam had hand-delivered a killer to their doorstep, then there would be a bad price to pay.

"I don't see Ramirez," Darcy said, her voice filled with nerves, her breath racing. She dropped to the floor, grabbed the laptop screen and moved closer, frantically studying it.

Nate looked, as well, and saw the same six screens he had earlier. All showed different parts of the ranch, including the front of the house, where Adam was parked. He didn't see Ramirez, either, but the thought had no sooner crossed his mind when white static filled the screen.

Hell.

"Ramirez," Darcy mumbled. "He did this?"

"Maybe." Nate sandwiched his cell between his shoulder and ear and sat next to Darcy. He took the laptop and typed in the security codes again to adjust the cameras.

Nothing.

"Ramirez jammed your security system, didn't he?"

Adam asked. The man didn't sound smug. He sounded as concerned as Nate felt. "He said he would. Said he had the equipment to do it. Now he can come after you, and you can't even see where he is."

"How do I know you didn't do this?" Nate fired back. "After all, you're the one who claims to have brought Ramirez here to the ranch." Nate mentally cursed when he tried the codes again. And they failed, again.

"It's not a claim. It's the truth," Adam insisted. "I had to bring him here or he would have killed me on the spot. He broke into my hotel room, put a gun to my head and forced me to drive him here. I couldn't just let him shoot me."

"He'll kill you, anyway," Nate pointed out.

He gave up on reactivating the exterior cameras and checked to make sure the intruder alarms for the doors and windows were still armed.

Thank God. They were.

"I'm not sitting out here in the open any longer," Adam said. "Ramirez could decide to come after me before he finishes you two off." At least that's what Nate thought the man said, but he couldn't be sure because Adam gunned the engine.

Darcy's gaze flew to his, and she started to get up from the floor, but Nate caught her shoulder to keep her where she was. Right now, the floor was the best place for her, especially since it meant she was away from the windows. The security system would trigger the alarms if anyone tried to break in, but Ramirez could still shoot through the glass.

"Adam's getting away," she reminded him.

"For now. And that's not a bad thing. I don't want to

have to deal with him right now. Only Ramirez." Besides, if Ramirez attempted to kill Adam, Nate would have to do something to stop it. He only wanted to concentrate on keeping Darcy and his brothers alive.

"We need another weapon," he said. He handed her his cell phone. "Stay put and call Mason to let him know what's going on. Tell him that Ramirez is probably headed straight for the house."

She gave a shaky nod, but her eyes widened when he handed her his gun. "It's just a precaution," he added. And maybe it would stay that way—a precaution—but Nate doubted it. Ramirez was a crazy man on a mission of murder.

He ran back down the hall while Darcy made the call to Mason. Nate tried to listen to the conversation, but thanks to the relentless storm, Darcy's voice soon faded from hearing range when he hurried into his office.

Where there were windows.

The windows were the reason he'd wanted Darcy to stay put.

Nate tried to make sure Ramirez wasn't lurking outside one of them, but the rain streaks on the glass and the darkness made it impossible. So, he stayed low and went to his desk. To the bottom drawer. It had a combination safety lock, and once again the darkness wasn't in his favor, but he finally entered the correct code and jerked open the drawer.

Two guns.

He slid one in his holster, held on to the other one and crammed some extra magazines of ammo into his pockets. It was more than enough to fight off one man, but Nate had no way of knowing if Ramirez had brought backup.

The moment Nate stepped back into the hall, his attention went to Darcy. She wasn't talking on the phone, but she was staring at the laptop screen.

"Did you get Mason?" he whispered. Also a precaution. Even though it was a long shot, he didn't want Ramirez to hear them and know where to shoot.

She nodded, still not taking her wide eyes from the screen. "Look," she insisted.

Nate cursed. He didn't have to guess that something was wrong. Darcy's expression said it all. And Nate soon knew what had caused her reaction.

Five of the security screens were still filled with static, but the sixth was working. Working, in a bad way.

Ramirez's face was on the screen.

He was clearly soaked, but he was giving them that slick grin that made Nate want to come through the computer and rid the man of his last breath.

"Can he see us?" Darcy asked.

"No." The security cameras didn't have a two-way feed. But Nate could certainly see Ramirez.

"Where is he? Can you tell?" she wanted to know.

Nate really hated to say this aloud. "I can't tell from the screen." Mainly, because Ramirez was blocking the entire camera. "It's camera five, and it's on this wing of the house."

"Oh, mercy," she mumbled.

And Nate had to agree. Ramirez had gone directly to the spot where they were, and Nate didn't think that was a coincidence. He studied the screen, looking for any sign that the man had an infrared device with him, but Nate could only see that face. That grin. And the evil in his eyes.

As a cop, Nate had faced cold-blooded killers before, but Ramirez was the worst of the worst.

"What's he saying?" Darcy asked when Ramirez's lips began to move.

There was no audio, but it didn't take Nate long to figure out that Ramirez was repeating the same three words.

Ready to die?

Judging from the gasp Darcy made, she had figured it out, as well.

"Mason said he'd let everyone know that Ramirez is on the grounds," Darcy relayed. "They're moving closer to the house so they can try to spot him."

Good. That meant in ten minutes or so, Darcy and he would have plenty of backup. Of course, Ramirez might have plenty, as well, and he needed to warn his brother that they might be walking into an ambush. Mason would already be prepared for that, but Nate wanted to make it crystal clear.

He took his phone back from Darcy. Just as Ramirez moved. Ramirez stepped to the side, and Nate then saw the other person behind Ramirez.

A man several yards away from the camera.

And this man wasn't a stranger. Far from it.

"What the heck is he doing here?" Darcy asked.

Nate cursed. He wanted to know the same damn thing.

WESLEY DENT'S FACE STARED back at Darcy.

But not for long. The screen went fuzzy again. A Ramirez mind game, no doubt. The man was trying to keep Nate and her off-kilter.

It was working.

Instead of focusing on the impending attack, Darcy was wondering what her former client was doing outside the ranch house with Ramirez. Was Dent there to try to kill them, too? And if so, why?

She tightened her grip on the gun and hoped she would have answers soon. So much for believing in Dent's innocence. He looked pretty darn guilty to her.

Crouched next to her, Nate flipped open his phone.

"You're calling Mason?" Darcy asked.

But Nate didn't have time to answer. Darcy heard the cracking sound and prayed it was a violent slash of lightning. But no. This was violence of a different kind.

A bullet slammed through a window.

Nate automatically shoved her lower to the floor, even though they weren't directly in front of the window. *Any* window. But it was certainly nearby because she could hear the broken glass clatter to the floor.

"The guest room," Nate supplied.

Her pulse kicked up a notch, and the blood rushed to her head. The guest room was where they'd made love less than a half hour earlier.

Nate made the call to Mason and warned him what was happening. The moment he ended the call, he moved her, positioning her behind him so that he was facing the side of house where that shot had been fired.

"Please tell me Mason is nearby," Darcy whispered.

"He's on his way."

On his way didn't seem nearly close enough, and yet she didn't want Mason or anyone else walking into gunfire.

The jolt of lightning lit up the hall, but the crashing

noise from the following thunder was minor compared to the next shot that slammed into the house.

More broken glass fell to the floor.

"That was also in the guest room," Nate explained. He took out an extra clip of ammo and handed it to her. "Just in case," he added.

That gave her another slam of adrenaline.

So did the next bullet.

No broken glass. Just a loud, deadly-sounding thud.

"It went through the wall," Nate whispered. She could hear the adrenaline in his voice, too, but his hand seemed steady.

Unlike hers.

Darcy was afraid she was shaking too hard to aim straight. The one good thing in all of this was that the children were safe. As bad as it was having Ramirez shoot at them, it would have been a million times worse if Kimmie and Noah had been anywhere nearby.

"Watch the foyer," Nate instructed, and he angled his body so that his aim was fastened to the guest-room door.

Darcy turned, as well, and watched, though it was hard to see anything in the pitch-black foyer. However, she was certain if Ramirez managed to come through the front door, then she would hear him. And the alarms would go off.

Another shot slammed through the wall.

Beside her, Nate's phone buzzed, and he answered it without taking his aim off the doorway. Since Darcy was so close, she could actually hear the person on the other end of the line.

Adam, again.

"You have to let me inside," Adam demanded. "I tried to leave, but someone fired a shot at me."

Darcy hadn't heard such a shot, but it could have happened far enough away that the storm could have drowned it out.

"Not a chance," Nate informed him. "We're under attack and going to the door to let you in would be suicide for all of us."

"Then what the hell am I supposed to do out here?" Adam yelled.

"My advice? Keep your voice down so Ramirez doesn't hear you. Then, find a place to take cover." Nate didn't wait for Adam to respond. He snapped his phone shut and crammed it back into his pocket.

Darcy wanted to ask if Nate thought Adam was in on this. Or Dent. But the next shot stopped her cold. Again, no broken glass. This was a heavy thudding sound, but in the murky darkness, she saw the drywall dust fly through the air.

Oh, no.

The shot hadn't gone through just the exterior of the wing, it had actually made it through the interior wall.

Just a few yards away from them.

She heard Nate's suddenly rough breath, and he glanced around as if trying to decide where to move. Any direction could be dangerous.

And the next bullet proved that.

The blast was louder, much louder than the others, and she saw the large hole it made in the hall wall.

Closer this time.

"Ramirez is using heavier artillery," Nate whispered. "Get all the way down on the floor."

But he didn't wait for her to do that. He put his hand

on her back and pushed her, hard, until her face was right against the hardwood.

Just as another bullet tore through the wall.

Sweet heaven. This one was even closer.

Maybe Ramirez was using infrared to find them, but if so, why hadn't he just aimed at them right from the beginning?

"Shhh," she heard Nate say, and he brushed the back of his hand over her cheek.

It took her a moment to realize he was doing that because her breathing was way too fast and shallow. She was on the verge of hyperventilating, and that couldn't happen. She couldn't fall apart because Nate needed her for backup in case Mason didn't get there in time.

Darcy concentrated on leveling her breath. And her heartbeat. She fixed her mind on Noah's smiling face. Kimmie's and Nate's, too, and just like that, her body started to settle down. She fought to hang on to her newly regained composure even when the next bullet slammed through the wall.

This one was just inches away.

"We have to move," Nate whispered, and he caught her arm.

Darcy wasn't even off the floor yet when there was another sound. Not a bullet this time.

Something much worse.

The security alarm blared, the noise seemingly shaking the walls. And she gasped. Because she knew what that sound meant.

Ramirez was inside the house.

Chapter Seventeen

Nate knew the nightmare had just gotten worse.

The clanging of the security alarms was deafening, but that wasn't his biggest concern. With that noise, he couldn't hear Ramirez or anyone else. And he needed to hear because in addition to Ramirez, he had both Adam and Dent on the grounds. For that matter, Marlene and Edwin could be at the ranch, as well.

Anything was possible.

Plus, he had to watch out for his brothers and everyone else trying to stop Ramirez.

Nate tried to keep watch all around them, but he had no idea where the intruder had entered. It could be any window or door in the house.

"I have to turn off the alarms," Nate shouted, though Darcy only shook her head and touched her fingers to her ear.

Nate grabbed her, lifted her from the floor and turned her to the side so she could keep watch at the back of the foyer. He would take the front door and the hall, the most likely point of entry since the shots had come from that direction.

Trying to make sure they weren't about to be ambushed, Nate led her into the foyer. Darcy kept her gun ready and aimed. Nate did the same. And they made their way across the open space.

Too open.

The sidelight windows around the door were especially worrisome because a gunman could fire right through those.

He held his breath, prayed and moved as fast as he could to the keypad panel on the wall between the foyer and the family room. His mind was racing. His heart, pounding. And it took several precious seconds to recall the code. The moment he punched in the numbers, the alarms went silent.

Nate lifted his head. Listened. The rain was battering against the door and windows, but he heard the wind, too. Not from the storm. This wind was whistling through the broken windows. He tried to pick through all those sounds so he could hear what he was listening for.

Footsteps.

They barely had time to register in his mind when a bullet slammed into the wall next to them. Darcy gasped and dived toward the family room. Nate was right behind her, and he fired in the direction of the shooter.

"You missed!" someone yelled out.

Ramirez.

It was true. The killer was inside.

As quietly as he could, Nate positioned Darcy behind the sofa. It wouldn't be much protection against bullets, but it was better than nothing. He cursed himself for this stupid bait plan and wondered how the devil he could get Darcy out of this alive. And how soon.

Where were Mason and the others?

Maybe someone had managed to nab Dent, Adam or anyone else outside waiting to help Ramirez.

Ramirez fired another shot at them. "You killed my brother," he shouted. "Did you really think I wouldn't make you pay for that?"

Nate didn't answer him. He didn't want Ramirez to use Nate's voice to pinpoint their position. However, Nate let his aim follow Ramirez's voice.

He sent another bullet toward the man.

Nate couldn't see him, but he was pretty sure he missed. Ramirez's laughter confirmed it. He'd moved. Maybe to the rear of the foyer?

If so, he was getting closer.

"Before I kill you," Ramirez shouted, "I think it's only fair I should tell you who hired me to kidnap your little brats."

Darcy's breath rattled, and she tried to come up from behind the sofa, but Nate pushed her right back down. He put his finger to his mouth in a stay-quiet warning. He hoped she realized that this was a trick that could get them killed, but he knew the firestorm Ramirez's offer had created inside her. She was afraid, yes, but like Nate, she wanted justice.

"Maybe you'd like me to take care of my boss before I punish you?" Ramirez asked.

The only thing Nate wanted was a name because when this was over, he would deal with that SOB, too. For now, though, he waited and listened for Ramirez to come into view. All Nate needed was one clean shot.

"Well?" Ramirez prompted.

There. In the deep shadows of the foyer, Nate saw what he'd been watching for. The silhouette of a man. He took aim. But before he could squeeze the trigger, there was god-awful sound of wood splintering, and the man ducked out of sight.

The door.

Someone had kicked it down.

Nate didn't fire because it could be one of his brothers, and because of that, he had to break his silence. "Ramirez is in the house!" Nate warned.

"What the hell?" Ramirez snarled.

And a shot tore through the foyer.

EVERYTHING SEEMED TO FREEZE, and Darcy felt the sickening dread slice through her.

The bullet wasn't the same as the others. There had been no sound of the metal ripping through drywall or glass.

No.

This was a deadly thud. Followed by a gasp. And Darcy knew. The bullet had been shot into *someone*.

She shoved her hand over her mouth so she couldn't cry out. This couldn't be happening. Ramirez couldn't have shot Mason or Kade. She couldn't be responsible for Nate losing anyone else in his life.

Darcy tried to get up, again, but once again Nate kept her pinned behind the sofa. "Stay put," he warned.

Nate, however, didn't heed his own warning. Neither did the person in the foyer because she heard footsteps. Someone was running, probably trying to escape.

With his gun aimed and his attention pinned to the foyer, Nate started walking. Slow, inch-by-inch steps. Darcy wanted to tell him to stop, but she couldn't. If one of his brothers was hurt or worse, then Nate would need to go to him. He would have to help. Or at least try.

It might be too late for help of any kind.

And then there was the flip side. Someone had already been shot, but Ramirez was still alive. Still armed. He would shoot Nate or anyone else if he got the chance, and that's when Darcy knew she couldn't obey Nate.

She had to help him.

Darcy eased up from behind the sofa and took aim in the same direction as Nate.

Nate mumbled some profanity, and that's when Darcy spotted the body on the foyer floor. She couldn't see the man's face because he was sprawled out on his stomach, but he was dressed all in black.

No. God, no.

Was it Mason?

Nate obviously thought it was his brother because she heard the shift in his breathing. Heard him whisper a prayer.

Darcy followed Nate to the edge of the foyer, but she waited, watching in case someone came through the now-open front door. Ramirez had perhaps gone out that way, but it didn't mean he wouldn't be back.

Nate inched closer, his gaze firing all around, and when he reached the body, he leaned down and touched his fingers to the man's neck. No cursing this time, but he groaned, a painful sound that tore right through her heart.

And he flipped the body over.

Nate froze for just a second, and Darcy started to go to him, to try to comfort him. But there wasn't time. He stood, and in the same motion, Nate whirled back around to face her.

Darcy shook her head, not understanding why he'd

done that. She didn't get a chance to ask because someone karate chopped her arm, causing her weapon to go flying through the air. But she felt another gun, cold and hard, when it was shoved against her back.

"Move and your boyfriend dies," the person behind her growled in a hoarse whisper.

Her breathing went crazy, started racing. As did her heart. And she looked past Nate's suddenly startled face and stared at the body on the foyer floor.

Not Mason.

It was Ramirez.

Darcy's stomach went to her knees. Because if Ramirez was there, lifeless and unmoving, then who had a gun jammed in her back?

"Sorry about this," the person whispered. It was a man, but she couldn't tell who. "You have to be my hostage for a little while."

Darcy had no intentions of being anyone's hostage.

She moved purely on instinct. She jerked away from her captor and dived to the side. But so did he, and he hooked his arm around her and held her in place. Still, she didn't give up. She didn't stop struggling.

Until the blast from a gun roared through her head.

Everything inside her went numb, and it took her a moment to realize she hadn't been shot. That it was the deafening noise from the bullet that had caused the pain to shoot through her. In fact, the gun hadn't even been aimed at her. The shot had been fired over her head.

"Darcy?" Nate called out.

She tried to answer him but couldn't get her throat unclamped. Darcy cursed her reaction and forced herself to move. She didn't intend to die without a fight so she rammed her elbow into her captor's stomach. It wasn't much, but it was enough for her to break the hold he had on her and scramble away.

She got just a glimpse of her attacker's face.

But a glimpse was all she needed to recognize him.

It was Adam.

He fired another shot, again over her head, and it slammed into the wall just a fraction of a second before he hooked his arm around her throat and put her in a choke hold.

Oh, mercy. She couldn't breathe. That caused panic to crawl through her. And worse, Nate was coming closer. Putting himself out in the open so that Adam could kill him, instead.

"Stop fighting me," Adam warned her. "Or Nate dies. Your choice."

That was no choice at all. She stopped fighting and prayed it would save Nate.

"Good girl," Adam whispered in a mock-sweet tone. But he did loosen the grip on her throat. Darcy frantically pulled in some much-needed air and hoped it was enough to stop her from passing out.

"Adam, give this up," Nate ordered. "You can't get out of here alive."

"No?" Adam answered. He kept his arm around her neck but aimed his gun at Nate. "So far, so good. Ramirez is dead."

"Yeah." With his own gun aimed at Adam, Nate inched closer, but he stayed in the foyer, out of Adam's direct line of fire. "You killed him before he could tell us that you were the one who hired him to set up the kidnapping."

Adam didn't deny it, and Darcy realized it was true.

Adam was the one who'd put the children in danger. Her fear was replaced by a jolt of anger.

How dare this moron do that!

"All this for money," Nate continued. He moved again. Just a fraction. And Darcy realized he was trying to get into a position so he could take Adam out.

Good. She wanted Adam to pay for what he'd done.

"Hey, it's always about money," Adam joked. He started inching toward the foyer. "If you'd just arrested Dent and tossed his sorry butt in jail, then my mother's estate would have been mine, and we wouldn't be here right now."

"But Dent isn't guilty," Nate concluded.

"No. But Dent is dead," Adam confessed. "I killed him about ten minutes ago."

Dead? Darcy tried hard to hang on to her composure. She was already losing that battle before Adam fired a shot into the foyer. She heard herself scream for Nate to get down, and somehow he managed to duck out of the way.

Adam cursed. "Move again, Lieutenant, and I'll shoot Darcy in the shoulder. It won't kill her, but it won't be fun, either." He shoved her forward, keeping his choke hold and his gun in place.

"Don't you have enough blood on your hands?" Nate asked. "First your mother with a lethal dose of insulin. Then, you kill Dent. Now, Ramirez. All of this to cover up what you've done. My theory? You knew what your mother had written in her diary so you tore out the page that would have incriminated you. But something happened, something that prevented you from destroying it."

"Yeah," Adam readily agreed, "and that was my

mother's fault. She saw me rip out the page, and she grabbed the diary and ran. She hid it before I found her and then wouldn't tell me where she'd put it. That's when I killed her."

Darcy could almost see it playing out. Sandra, terrified of her own son as he shoved a needle into her arm. She understood that terror because she was feeling it now.

"Unless you do something to ruin my plan," Adam went on, "the diary is what will keep you both alive."

"What do you mean?" Darcy asked.

But Adam didn't answer her. He nailed his attention to Nate. "I want you to give me the diary so I can destroy it."

"Impossible," Nate fired back.

"No. It's doable for a man in your position. I'll take Darcy someplace safe while you go to the crime lab. When you bring me the diary, then I'll let Darcy go. Well, after I've cashed in my mother's estate and escaped, of course."

The adrenaline and the anger were making it hard for her to think, but Darcy could still see the faulty logic. Adam wouldn't let them go. If he got his hands on the diary and Sandra's money, he would kill them so he could cover up his crimes.

Or rather, he'd try to kill them.

"There's no need to take Darcy," Nate bargained. "I can call and have the diary brought to us."

She latched on to that, hoping Adam would agree. If they could somehow prevent him from leaving the ranch with her, then she would have a better chance of escape.

But Adam shook his head.

"Not a chance. As long as I have Darcy, you'll do whatever it takes to cooperate." Adam tightened his grip on her and muscled her into the foyer and toward the front door. "Lieutenant, tell your brothers and anybody else out there to back off." He shoved Darcy forward again, toward the door.

Nate's gaze slashed from Adam's gun to her own eyes, and she saw the raw, painful emotions there. Nate was blaming himself for this. She wanted to tell him that it wasn't his fault. But there was no time to tell him anything. Because Adam dragged her out onto the porch, down the steps and toward his car, which was parked behind Nate's SUV. Adam had obviously pretended to drive away from the ranch.

The storm came right at her, assaulting her. The rain stung her eyes, but that didn't stop her from seeing the shadowy figure on the side of the house.

Mason.

He had his gun drawn, like Nate, who was now in the doorway, but neither could fire. The way Adam was holding her would make it next to impossible for either of them to get a clean shot.

"Lieutenant, tell your brother to back off," Adam warned, forcing Darcy into the yard.

But Mason stepped out. "She makes a lousy hostage," Mason snarled. "She's a good six inches shorter than you, and that means somebody out here has a good chance at a head shot. *Your* head."

She felt Adam's arm tense, and he crouched farther down behind her. Maybe Kade or one of the others was behind them, but that still didn't mean there'd be a clean shot. After all, the bullet could go through Adam and into her.

"I'd make a better human shield," Mason offered. He shrugged as if he didn't have a care in the world. "I'll take her place."

Part of her was touched that Mason would even make the offer, but she didn't want to place Nate's brother in even more danger. Apparently neither did Nate because he inched down the steps.

"What a dilemma, Lieutenant," Adam mocked. He clucked his tongue. "Your brother or your lover. So, which one will it be?"

Oh, mercy. Darcy hadn't thought this could get any worse, but she'd been wrong. It was sick to force Nate into making a choice like this.

"It's okay," Darcy insisted. "I'll go with him." Well, she would, but she would also try to escape. She wasn't about to give up.

"No, you won't go with him," Nate said. "If Adam won't take me, then Mason will go."

Adam made a sound of amusement. "You're choosing her over your own blood?"

Nate gave him a look that could have frozen Hades. "Mason's a cop. Darcy's a civilian."

Mason just shrugged again and then nodded.

Adam didn't respond right away, and she couldn't see his expression. However, she could feel his muscles tense again. "No deal," Adam finally said. "She'll be a lot easier to control than either of you. Besides, Darcy knows if she doesn't cooperate, I'll just go after her son again."

It took a few seconds for those words to sink in, and they didn't sink in well. How dare this SOB threaten Noah again.

Her hands tightened to fists.

And that was for starters.

The slam of anger created a new jolt of adrenaline, and it wasn't just her hands that tightened. The rest of her body did, too. Suddenly, she was primed and ready for a fight and needed someplace to aim all this dangerous energy boiling inside her.

She saw the anger—no, make that *rage*—go through Nate's eyes, and she knew he was within seconds of launching himself at Adam. That couldn't happen because Adam would shoot him. But maybe there was something she could do to improve Nate's odds.

Darcy frantically looked around her. There was nothing nearby that she could grab. No shrubs, rocks or weapons. But the car was directly behind them, and Darcy watched. And waited.

Until Adam reached to open the door.

She used every bit of her anger and adrenaline when she drew back her elbow and rammed it into Adam's ribs. He sputtered out a cough and eased up on his grip just enough to give her some room to maneuver. Darcy lifted her foot, put her weight behind it and punched her heel into his shin.

"Get down!" Nate yelled to her.

Darcy had already started to do just that, but Adam latched on to her hair. The pain shot through her, but she kicked him again. And again. Fighting to get loose from him.

She succeeded.

Darcy fell facedown onto the slick driveway, the rough, wet concrete grating across her knees and forearms. She immediately tried to scramble for cover behind the car.

But it was too late for that.

From the corner of her eye, she saw Adam lift his gun. Take aim.

And he fired.

Chapter Eighteen

Nate felt the searing pain slice through him.

Just like that, his legs gave way, and he had no choice but to drop to the ground.

Hell.

Adam had shot him.

That, and the pain, registered in his mind, and he maneuvered his gun so he could try to protect Darcy. He had to stop Adam from taking her.

Or worse.

The sound of another gunshot let him know that worse could have already happened.

"Darcy?" Nate managed to call out.

She didn't answer, and he couldn't see her, but there was the sound of chaos all around him.

Another shot.

Mason shouted something that was drowned out by the thunder, and suddenly there was movement. Footsteps. Some kind of scuffle. A sea of people—FBI agents and the ranch hands. All of them converged on Adam and took him to the ground.

"Darcy?" Nate yelled.

He had to make sure she was safe. He had to see for himself. If Adam had managed to shoot her... But he couldn't go there. Couldn't even think it. Because he was responsible for this.

No.

It was more than that.

Nate couldn't lose her. It was as simple as that. He couldn't lose her because he loved her.

He would have laughed if it hadn't been for the god-awful pain searing his left shoulder. It was a really bad time to realize just how he felt about Darcy.

"Nate?" he heard someone say.

He lifted his head and amid that swarm of people, he saw her. Darcy. She had mud on her face and clothes, and he couldn't tell if she'd been shot. But she was moving.

Or rather, running.

She hurried to him and pulled him into her arms. He saw the blood then and had a moment of rage where he wanted to tear Adam limb from limb.

But then he noticed that the blood was his.

Thank God. Darcy was all right.

"You're hurt," she said, her voice shaking almost violently.

Yeah, he was, but that didn't matter now. "Are you okay?"

"No." She made a sobbing sound, and her tears slid through the mud on her cheeks. "I'm not okay because you've been shot."

Oh. That. The relief didn't help with his pain, but it helped with everything else.

Darcy was okay.

Adam hadn't managed to shoot her, after all.

"Can you stand?" she asked. "I don't want to wait for an ambulance. I'll drive you to the hospital."

Nate hated the worry in her eyes. Hated those tears. But he couldn't refuse her offer. Even he wasn't too stubborn to refuse a trip to the hospital—though he did want to first make sure that Adam had been neutralized. Nate glanced around, but he couldn't tell. Because he couldn't actually see the man who'd just tried to kill him.

However, he did see Mason.

His brother broke from the group and made a beeline for him. "Hurt much?" Mason asked. But he didn't wait for an answer. With Darcy on one side of him and Mason on the other, they got Nate to his feet and headed toward his SUV.

"What about Adam?" Nate wanted to know.

"Kade is on him." Mason glanced back at the huddle of activity. "Literally. He's not going anywhere except to jail."

Good. One less thing to worry about right now. Later, he would deal with his hatred for this SOB who'd nearly cost Nate everything.

Darcy pressed her hand to his shoulder, right where it was burning like fire, but he guessed she was doing that to stop the blood flow and not to make him wince in pain.

"Are you okay?" Darcy whispered as they hauled Nate onto the backseat of the SUV. Darcy followed right in beside him and crouched on the floor. Mason peeled out of the driveway, the tires of the SUV kicking up gravel and rain.

"I'm okay," Nate tried.

"Are you really?" she questioned.

Since she sounded very close to losing it, Nate decided to give her some reassurance. He slid his hand around the back of her neck, pulled her to him and kissed her. He wasn't surprised when it gave him some reassurance, too.

"Can't be hurt that bad if you can do that to her," Mason growled.

"I'm not hurt that bad," Nate verified. And he was almost certain that was true. It was hard to tell through the blistering pain.

"You were shot," Darcy pointed out. The frantic tone was back in her voice. "Adam could have killed you."

"He could have killed you, too," Nate reminded her.

But it was a reminder that cut him right across the heart. He would see Adam in his nightmares. Darcy would, too. And Nate would never forgive Adam for that and for placing Noah and Kimmie in grave danger.

"Adam got some blood on his hands tonight," Mason said, his attention glued to the wet road. The wipers slashed across the windshield. "I'm the one who found Dent just a few seconds before he died from a gunshot wound to the chest. He told me Adam had called him to come to the ranch and said that he had proof it was Edwin who'd killed Sandra."

Dent had been stupid to fall for that, but then Adam had probably convinced him that he'd be safe at the ranch with a cop, an FBI agent and a deputy sheriff.

"What about Ramirez's partner?" Nate asked. "Someone needs to make sure he doesn't try to help Adam."

"He can't help anybody," Mason assured him. "Right before Adam grabbed Darcy, Kade found Ramirez's partner—dead."

Adam, no doubt. With Ramirez and Sandra Dent, that meant Adam had killed at least three, maybe four people. A lot of murder and mayhem all for the sake of money. But the high body count along with the kidnapping charges meant there was no way Adam could escape the death penalty.

"How much longer before we get to the hospital?" Darcy asked.

"Not long," Mason assured her. "One of the ranch hands is calling ahead so the E.R. will be expecting us."

She kept her hand pressed over his wound and kept mumbling something. A prayer, he realized.

"The pain's not that bad," he lied.

But more of her tears came, anyway, and they were followed by a heart-wrenching sob. "I should have held on to Adam's arm. I should have kicked him harder." Darcy shook her head. "I should have done something to stop him from firing that gun."

"Hey, don't do this." Nate touched her chin and lifted it. "I'm the one who planned for us to be bait."

"The plan worked," Darcy reminded him, though she had to draw in a deep breath before saying it. "What didn't work was that I allowed Adam to take me at gunpoint. That's when things went wrong."

He could have told her that things went wrong when Adam killed his mother, but Nate didn't think Darcy would hear the logic. No, she was hurting and worried, and he was the cause of that.

Nate hoped he could also be the cure.

He pulled her back to him for another kiss. And another. And he kept it up until oxygen became a big concern for both of them. But he figured he might need her a little breathless for what he was about to say.

"I don't want to lose you," he let her know.

She shook her head, smeared the tears from her

cheeks. "Adam isn't a threat anymore. Nor Ramirez. We'll be safe."

Yeah. But that wasn't where Nate was going with this. "I don't want to lose you," he repeated.

Darcy blinked. Shook her head again.

"Part of me will always love Ellie," he explained. "But I can't live in the past, and she was my past...."

"We're here," Mason announced, and he braked to a screeching halt directly in front of the E.R. door.

Nate choked back the pain that was blurring his vision and gathered his breath. He wanted to finish this now.

"Darcy, will you marry me?"

She opened her mouth, but nothing came out. *Nothing.* And then the moment was gone.

Everything started to move way too fast. Two medics threw open the SUV's door and hauled him onto a gurney. Nate got one last glimpse of Darcy's startled, bleached face before the medics whisked him away.

DARCY WAS AFRAID if she sat down, she'd collapse. So, she kept pacing and waiting. Something she'd been doing for nearly an hour. It felt more like an eternity.

"SAPD is booking Adam right now," Mason relayed to her from the chair in the corner of the waiting room. He had his feet stretched out in front of him as if he were lounging, and he'd been on and off the phone— mainly on—since they'd arrived at the E.R.

Mason certainly didn't seem crazy scared, like she did. But then, neither did Dade, who had his shoulder propped against the wall. He, too, was on the phone, with his fiancée, and from the sound of it, both Kayla and Grayson's wife, Eve, were on their way to the hospital to see Nate. Kade was the only Ryland who showed signs of stress. He was seated, elbows on knees, his face buried in his hands.

"What about Marlene and Edwin?" Darcy asked. Because it occurred to her if Adam had killed Dent, his mother and Ramirez, he might have killed others.

"They're safe and sound," Mason answered. "Neither appears to have had anything to do with this. According to Mel, Edwin's pretty torn up."

Of course. His son would be facing the death penalty.

"Adam was chatty when he arrived at the sheriff's office," Mason went on. "He admitted to trying to make his father look guilty. He wanted the blame placed on anyone but him. Edwin might not be so torn up when he learns that sonny boy was willing to let him take the fall for murder." Mason's phone buzzed again.

Darcy continued to pace until she heard Mason mention Grayson's name, and that stopped her. She certainly hadn't forgotten about the children, but with Nate's injury, she'd put him at the top of her worry list.

Until now.

She hoped Grayson wasn't phoning because there was a problem. She moved closer to him so she could try to hear, but the call ended quickly.

"Grayson and the kids are on their way here," Mason relayed. "Everybody's okay."

The blood rushed to her head. A mix of relief and happiness overcame her when she realized she would soon get to see Noah and Kimmie. But Darcy knew there wouldn't be total relief until she saw Nate. Until she talked to him.

Until she asked him about that *question*.

Heaven knows how long that would be. Besides, he might not even know what he'd said. Nate had been in so much pain, and mixed with the blood loss and the shock, he might have been talking out of his head.

Everything suddenly felt still and silent. None of the Rylands were on their phones. Like her, they were fully in the wait mode. Except for Mason. He was studying her with those intense, steely eyes.

"Well?" he asked.

Darcy froze. Because even though that one word hardly qualified as a question, she was positive what Mason meant. After all, Mason had been in that SUV, and he'd almost certainly heard Nate's question.

Kade lifted his head. Looked at Mason. Then at her. "Well what?"

Oh, no. She hadn't wanted to do this tonight and especially not before she'd had a chance to speak with Nate.

But apparently Mason did. "Right before the medics took him into the E.R., Nate asked Darcy to marry him."

The room was suddenly so quiet that Darcy could hear her own heartbeat. It was racing.

All three Rylands stared at her. And stared. But it was Dade who walked toward her. He stopped just a few inches away, and she braced herself for a good tongue-lashing about how she'd played on Nate's vulnerability.

"What was your answer?" Dade asked.

She managed to shrug, somehow, though her muscles seemed frozen in place. "There wasn't time for an answer."

Dade waited, still staring, and it became clear that he expected her to reveal what that answer would be.

"I want to tell Nate first," she explained. And she braced herself for Dade to demand to know.

But he reached out, put his arm around her and eased her to him. He brushed a kiss on her forehead. "I hope you'll say yes."

Darcy couldn't have been any more stunned. "You do?"

The corner of his mouth lifted, probably because all that shock had made it into her voice. "You're good for Nate."

Kade stood, crammed his hands in his pockets and walked closer, as well. "You are good for him," he verified. "It's nice to see Nate happy for a change."

Again, she got another dose of being stunned. "I'm in love with him," she blurted out. *Oh, mercy.* She hadn't expected to say that. Not to them, anyway.

"Does he know that?" Dade asked.

Darcy shook her head, causing Kade and Dade to grumble under their breaths. "You need to tell him," Dade insisted.

She would. Once she could speak. And once she got past the whole "maybe Nate was talking out of his head" thing. Maybe he wouldn't remember proposing to her.

"I hope like the devil that you two get married the same time as Kayla and Dade," Mason mumbled. "No way do I want to wear a monkey suit twice."

Kade huffed. "Ignore Mr. Congeniality over there. You name the date for him to be in a monkey suit, and he'll be in one. There are four of us and one of him."

Mason matched that huff. "Yeah, and it'll take all

four of you weenies to try." He sounded serious enough, but Darcy suspected he was joking.

She was about to ask for clarification, but the door behind them swung open.

And there was Nate.

His shirt was open, exposing the bandage on his shoulder, and his left arm was in a pristine-white sling. He looked exhausted. And really confused when his gaze landed on all of them.

Darcy hurried to him, slipped her arms around his waist and tried to give him a gentle hug. "You're okay?" she asked. And she cursed the tears that came automatically.

"I am," Nate verified. "The bullet went straight through. No real damage. The doctor says I'll be fine in about a week or so."

Now, here was the flood of relief that she'd waited for. Nate was all right.

He brushed a kiss on her cheek and ducked down to make eye contact. "Is something, uh, wrong?"

"No," Darcy jumped to answer. Unfortunately, Dade and Kade jumped to answer with their own noes.

Mason just made a snorting sound. "I told them about your marriage proposal. And Darcy told us that she's in love with you." He looked at Nate. "Yeah, we were surprised, too. We didn't consider you, well, all that lovable."

That brought on some snickers from Kade and Dade, but Nate just kept looking at her. "Did you tell them the answer to my proposal?"

Suddenly all eyes were on her again. "No. I said I needed to talk to you first."

Nate's face dropped, and around her she heard the

murmurings of the Ryland brothers as they started to leave, giving them some time alone to absorb what she was about to say. Of course, judging from the sudden mood in the room, they thought she was about to say no.

So, Darcy tried one of Nate's ploys.

She kissed him. She didn't keep it exactly gentle, either. It was best if he knew just how deep, and how hot, her feelings were for him. She didn't break the mouth-to-mouth contact until Mason cleared his throat, a reminder that Nate and she weren't alone, after all.

Darcy eased back and looked Nate in the eyes. "I'm in love with you."

Nate smiled that little smile that made her want to kiss him again. And haul him off to bed.

But bed could wait.

"Yes," she added. "I want to marry you."

Nate's smile suddenly wasn't so little. "Good. Because I'm in love with you, and I definitely want to marry you." He hooked his uninjured arm around her and hauled her closer to him for a perfect kiss.

One that caused Dade and Kade to whoop.

Nate and she broke away laughing. And then kissed again.

Darcy hadn't thought this moment could get any better, but then she heard the familiar voices. Grayson was making his way toward them, and he was carrying both babies. Amazingly, both were wide-awake and were squirming to get down. Grayson eased them both onto the floor, and the two toddled into the waiting area.

"Here," Kade said, peeling off his jacket and slipping it on Darcy.

That's when Darcy realized she had blood on her top. Nate's blood. And she didn't want the children to see that. "Thank you," she whispered to Kade.

"Anything for my new sister-in-law." He brushed a kiss on her cheek and moved away so she could kneel down and give both babies a big hug.

Kimmie started babbling as though trying to tell Darcy all about their adventure at the safe house, and Darcy scooped up both of them so that Nate wouldn't have to bend down for all-around kisses.

"Boo-boo," Noah announced when he spotted the bandage on Nate's shoulder, and when he kissed it, Kimmie repeated the syllables and kissed it, as well.

"Your mom and I are getting married," Nate told Noah. "How do you feel about that?"

Noah looked pensive for a moment, then grinned and babbled some happy sounds.

Her son was obviously okay with this. "And what do you think?" Darcy asked Kimmie.

Kimmie looked at her uncle Mason. "Your call, curly locks," he told her.

Even though there was no way Kimmie knew what that meant, she giggled and clapped her hands.

Darcy had never thought she could feel this much happiness, but then she saw Grayson, the only person in the room who hadn't given some kind of thumbs-up. She wouldn't take back her yes. She loved Nate too much to walk away because his brother disapproved, but she wanted it just the same.

"I'm in love with Nate," Darcy told Grayson, just in case he'd missed that part.

Grayson nodded. "Then I guess that leaves me with

just one thing to say." He leaned in and brushed a kiss on her cheek. "Welcome to the family."

A breath of relief swooshed out of her, causing Kimmie to laugh and try to make the same sound. Darcy looked at Nate and saw the love he had for all of them.

Nate kissed her despite the fact he had to maneuver through both kids to do that. "Ready to go home?" he whispered against her mouth.

Darcy didn't even have to consider this answer. "Yes."

And with Nate's arm around her, they took their first step toward their new life together.

* * * * *

SUSPENSE

Heartstopping stories of intrigue and mystery—
where true love always triumphs.

COMING NEXT MONTH
AVAILABLE FEBRUARY 14 2012

HICNM0112

REQUEST YOUR FREE BOOKS!
2 FREE NOVELS PLUS 2 FREE GIFTS!

◆ **Harlequin**°

INTRIGUE°

BREATHTAKING ROMANTIC SUSPENSE

YES! Please send me 2 FREE Harlequin Intrigue® novels and my 2 FREE gifts (gifts are worth about $10). After receiving them, if I don't wish to receive any more books, I can return the shipping statement marked "cancel." If I don't cancel, I will receive 6 brand-new novels every month and be billed just $4.49 per book in the U.S. or $5.24 per book in Canada. That's a saving of at least 14% off the cover price! It's quite a bargain! Shipping and handling is just 50¢ per book in the U.S. and 75¢ per book in Canada.* I understand that accepting the 2 free books and gifts places me under no obligation to buy anything. I can always return a shipment and cancel at any time. Even if I never buy another book, the two free books and gifts are mine to keep forever.

182/382 HDN FEQ2

Name _____ (PLEASE PRINT) _____

Address _____ Apt. # _____

City _____ State/Prov. _____ Zip/Postal Code _____

Signature (if under 18, a parent or guardian must sign)

Mail to the Reader Service:
IN U.S.A.: P.O. Box 1867, Buffalo, NY 14240-1867
IN CANADA: P.O. Box 609, Fort Erie, Ontario L2A 5X3

Not valid for current subscribers to Harlequin Intrigue books.

**Are you a subscriber to Harlequin Intrigue books
and want to receive the larger-print edition?
Call 1-800-873-8635 or visit www.ReaderService.com.**

* Terms and prices subject to change without notice. Prices do not include applicable taxes. Sales tax applicable in N.Y. Canadian residents will be charged applicable taxes. Offer not valid in Quebec. This offer is limited to one order per household. All orders subject to credit approval. Credit or debit balances in a customer's account(s) may be offset by any other outstanding balance owed by or to the customer. Please allow 4 to 6 weeks for delivery. Offer available while quantities last.

Your Privacy—The Reader Service is committed to protecting your privacy. Our Privacy Policy is available online at www.ReaderService.com or upon request from the Reader Service.

We make a portion of our mailing list available to reputable third parties that offer products we believe may interest you. If you prefer that we not exchange your name with third parties, or if you wish to clarify or modify your communication preferences, please visit us at www.ReaderService.com/consumerschoice or write to us at Reader Service Preference Service, P.O. Box 9062, Buffalo, NY 14269. Include your complete name and address.

HI11B

*Louisa Morgan loves being around children.
So when she has the opportunity to tutor bedridden Ellie,
she's determined to bring joy back into the motherless
girl's world. Can she also help Ellie's father open his
heart again? Read on for a sneak peek of*

THE COWBOY FATHER

*by Linda Ford,
available February 2012 from Love Inspired Historical.*

Why had Louisa thought she could do this job? A bubble of self-pity whispered she was totally useless, but Louisa ignored it. She wasn't useless. She could help Ellie if the child allowed it.

Emmet walked her out, waiting until they were out of earshot to speak. "I sense you and Ellie are not getting along."

"Ellie has lost her freedom. On top of that, everything is new. Familiar things are gone. Her only defense is to exert what little independence she has left. I believe she will soon tire of it and find there are more enjoyable ways to pass the time."

He looked doubtful. Louisa feared he would tell her not to return. But after several seconds' consideration, he sighed heavily. "You're right about one thing. She's lost everything. She can hardly be blamed for feeling out of sorts."

"She hasn't lost everything, though." Her words were quiet, coming from a place full of certainty that Emmet was more than enough for this child. "She has you."

"She'll always have me. As long as I live." He clenched his fists. "And I fully intend to raise her in such a way that even if something happened to me, she would never feel like I was gone. I'd be in her thoughts and in her actions every day."

Peace filled Louisa. "Exactly what my father did."

Their gazes connected, forged a single thought about fathers and daughters…how each needed the other. How sweet the relationship was.

Louisa tipped her head away first. "I'll see you tomorrow."

Emmet nodded. "Until tomorrow then."

She climbed behind the wheel of their automobile and turned toward home. She admired Emmet's devotion to his child. It reminded her of the love her own father had lavished on Louisa and her sisters. Louisa smiled as fond memories of her father filled her thoughts. Ellie was a fortunate child to know such love.

Louisa understands what both father and daughter are going through. Will her compassion help them heal—and form a new family? Find out in
THE COWBOY FATHER
by Linda Ford, available February 14, 2012.

Love Inspired Books celebrates 15 years of inspirational romance in 2012! February puts the spotlight on Love Inspired Historical, with each book celebrating family and the special place it has in our hearts. Be sure to pick up all four Love Inspired Historical stories, available February 14, wherever books are sold.

Harlequin® Super Romance®

Discover a touching new trilogy from
USA TODAY bestselling author

Janice Kay Johnson

Between Love and Duty

As the eldest brother of three, Duncan MacLachlan
is used to being in control and maintaining an
emotional distance; as a police captain it's his job.
But when he meets Jane Brooks, Duncan soon finds
his control slipping away. Together, they fight for a
young boy's future, and soon Duncan finds himself
hoping to build a future with Jane.

Available February 2012

From Father to Son
(March 2012)

The Call of Bravery
(April 2012)

Harlequin *Blaze*

red-hot reads

Rhonda Nelson

SIZZLES WITH ANOTHER INSTALLMENT OF

When former ranger Jack Martin is assigned to
provide security to Mariette Levine, a local pastry
chef, he believes this will be an open-and-shut case.
Yet the danger becomes all too real when Mariette is
attacked. But things aren't always what they seem,
and soon Jack's protective instincts demand he save
the woman he is quickly falling for.

THE KEEPER

**Available February 2012
wherever books are sold.**